Chainsaw Earle

Written by **Kevin Blackmore** and **Wayne Chaulk,**
Buddy Wasisname and the Other Fellers

Illustrations by **Kevin Tobin**

CREATIVE PUBLISHERS

St. John's, NL 2011

Canada Council for the Arts | Conseil des Arts du Canada | Canada | Newfoundland Labrador

We gratefully acknowledge the financial support of the Canada Council for the Arts, the Government of Canada through the Canada Book Fund (CBF), and the Government of Newfoundland and Labrador through the Department of Tourism, Culture and Recreation for our publishing program.

Cover Design and Layout by Kevin Tobin
Illustrations by Kevin Tobin
Printed on acid-free paper

Published by
CREATIVE PUBLISHERS
an imprint of CREATIVE BOOK PUBLISHING
a Transcontinental Inc. associated company
P.O. Box 8660, Stn. A
St. John's, Newfoundland and Labrador A1B 3T7

Printed in Canada by:
TRANSCONTINENTAL INC.

Library and Archives Canada Cataloguing in Publication

Blackmore, Kevin
Chainsaw Earle / written by Kevin Blackmore and Wayne Chaulk, Buddy Wasisname and the Other Fellers ; illustrations by Kevin Tobin.

ISBN 978-1-897174-82-1

I. Chaulk, Wayne II. Buddy Wasisname and the Other Fellers III. Tobin, Kevin, 1958- IV. Title.

PS8603.L2759C53 2011 C813'.6 C2011-905312-8

FSC
www.fsc.org
MIX
Paper from responsible sources
FSC® C011825

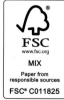

Stunned as we are, we are not so stunned as to fail to appreciate all the stunned people who supported three stunned arses during our 28 years as Buddy Wasisname And The Other Fellers. This book is dedicated to you.

– Wayne, Kevin, Ray

To my Mother-in-law. Cavell, thanks for everything. You are like a smokin' hot 2002 Pontiac Sunfire. And they don't make them like that any more.

– KT.

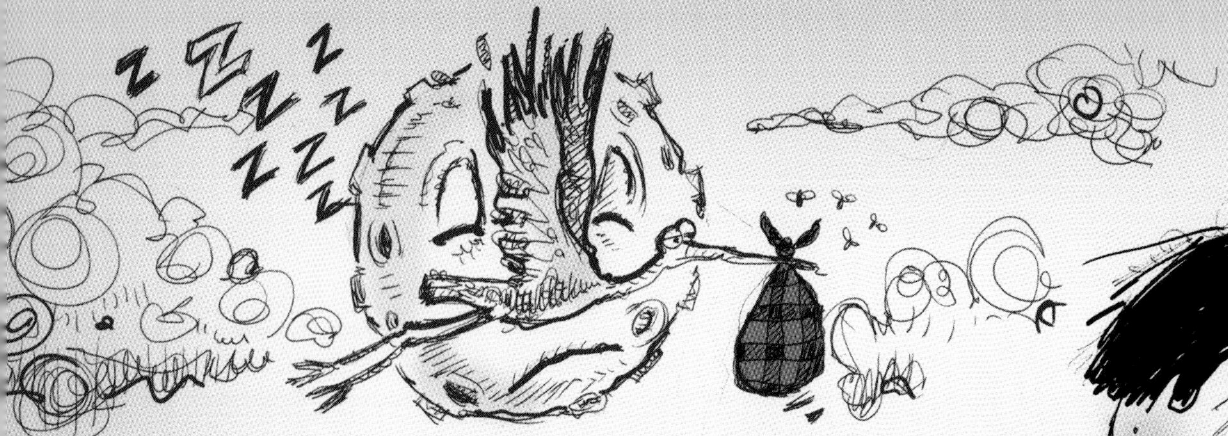

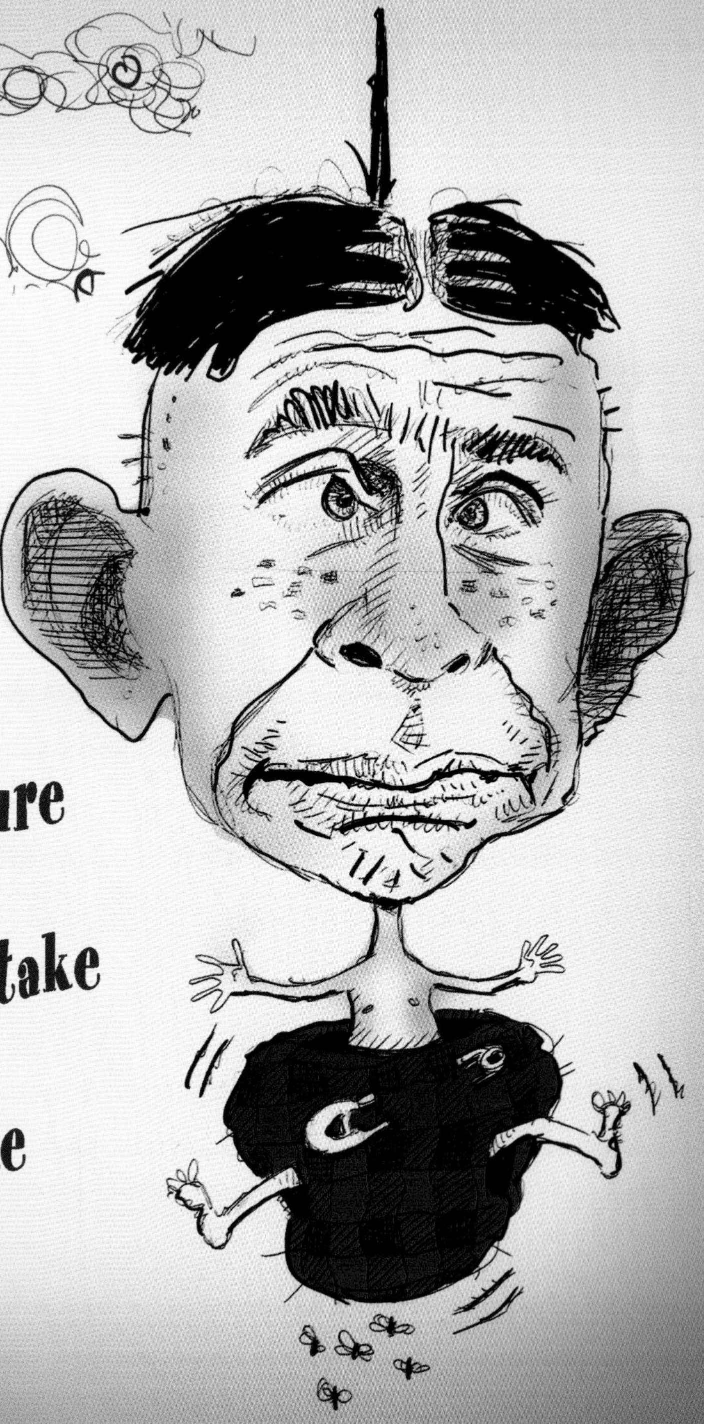

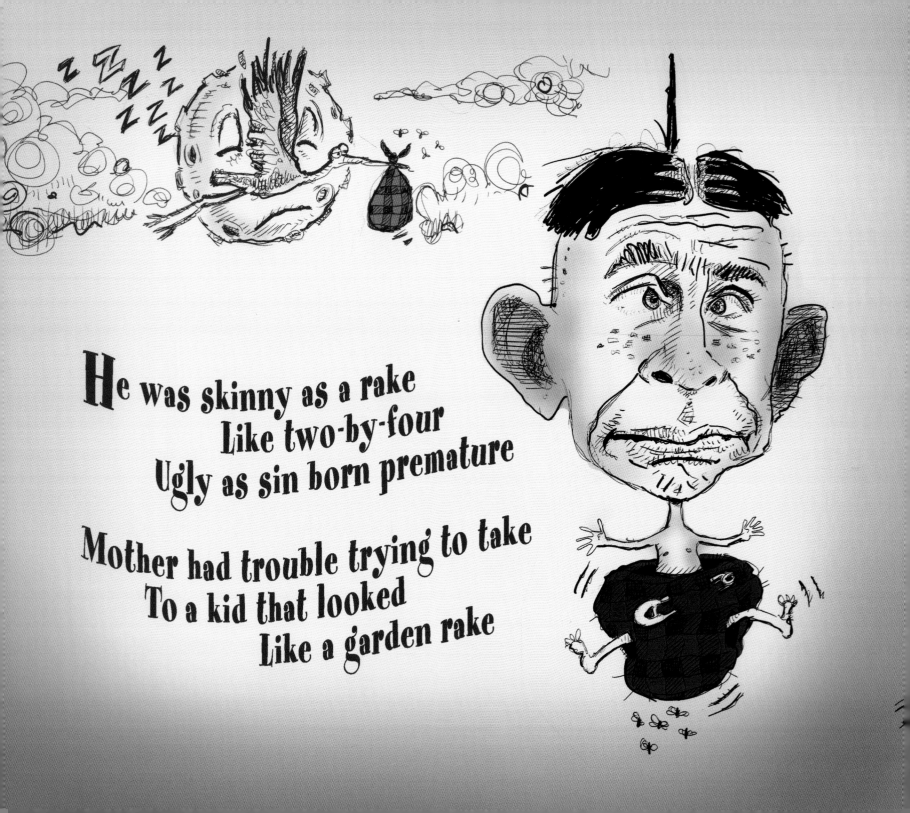

He was skinny as a rake
Like two-by-four
Ugly as sin born premature

Mother had trouble trying to take
To a kid that looked
Like a garden rake

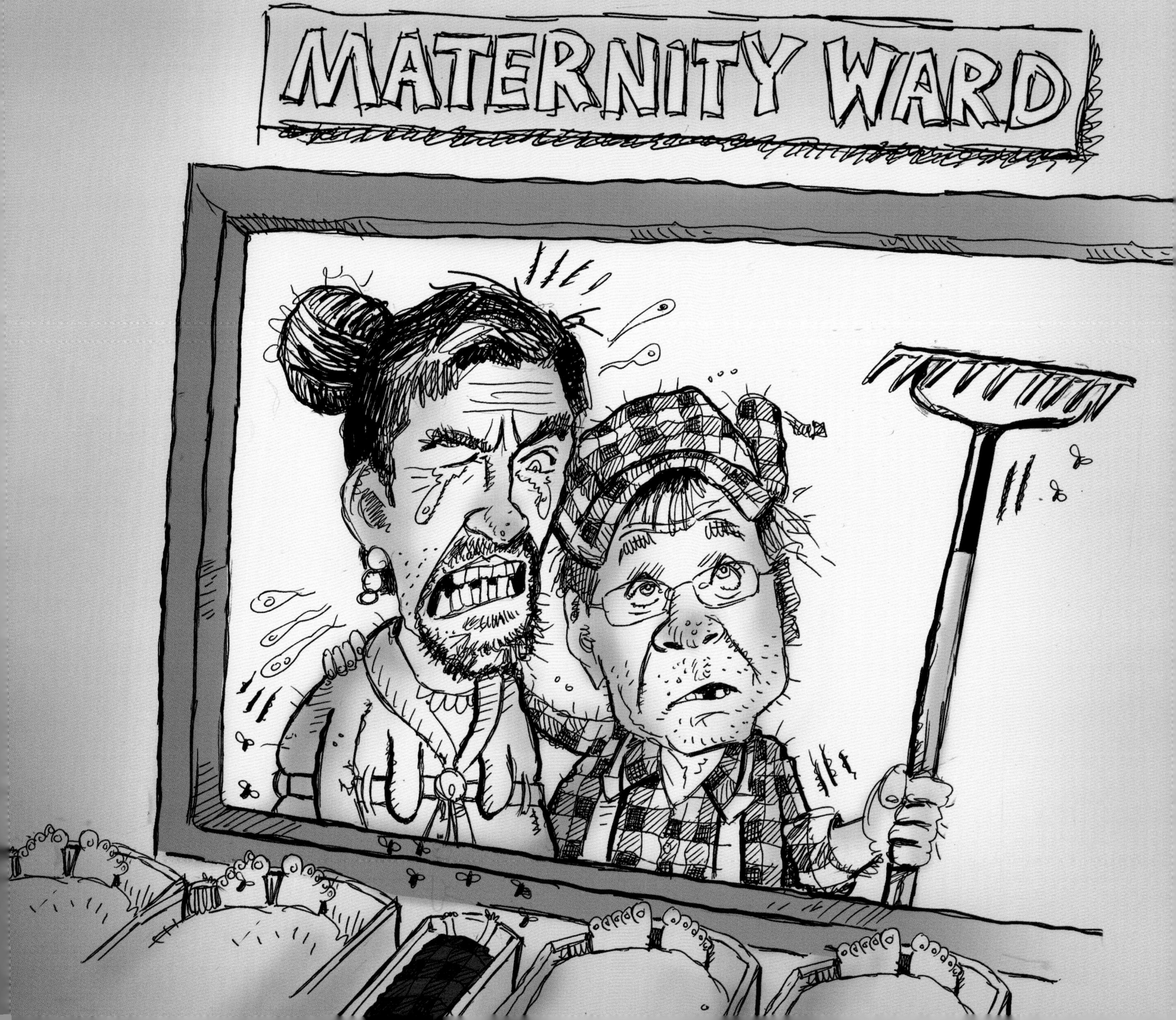
MATERNITY WARD

But, sons are sons... and Dad wasn't proud
Didn't make him feel like one of the crowd
Wood-cuttin' boys from up in the sticks
Laughed at the sight of Earle

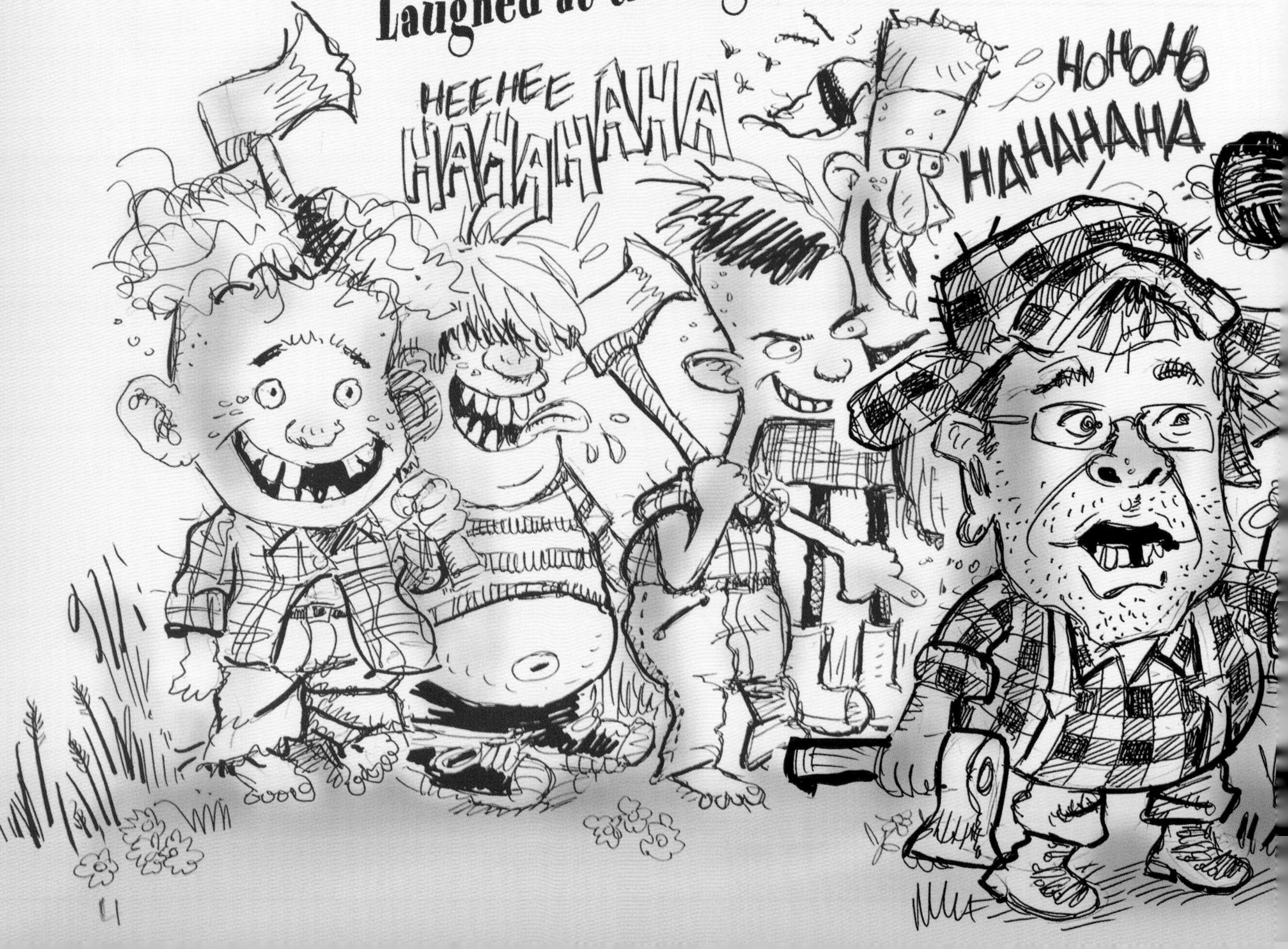
HEEHEE
HAHAHAHA
HOHOHO
HAHAHAHA

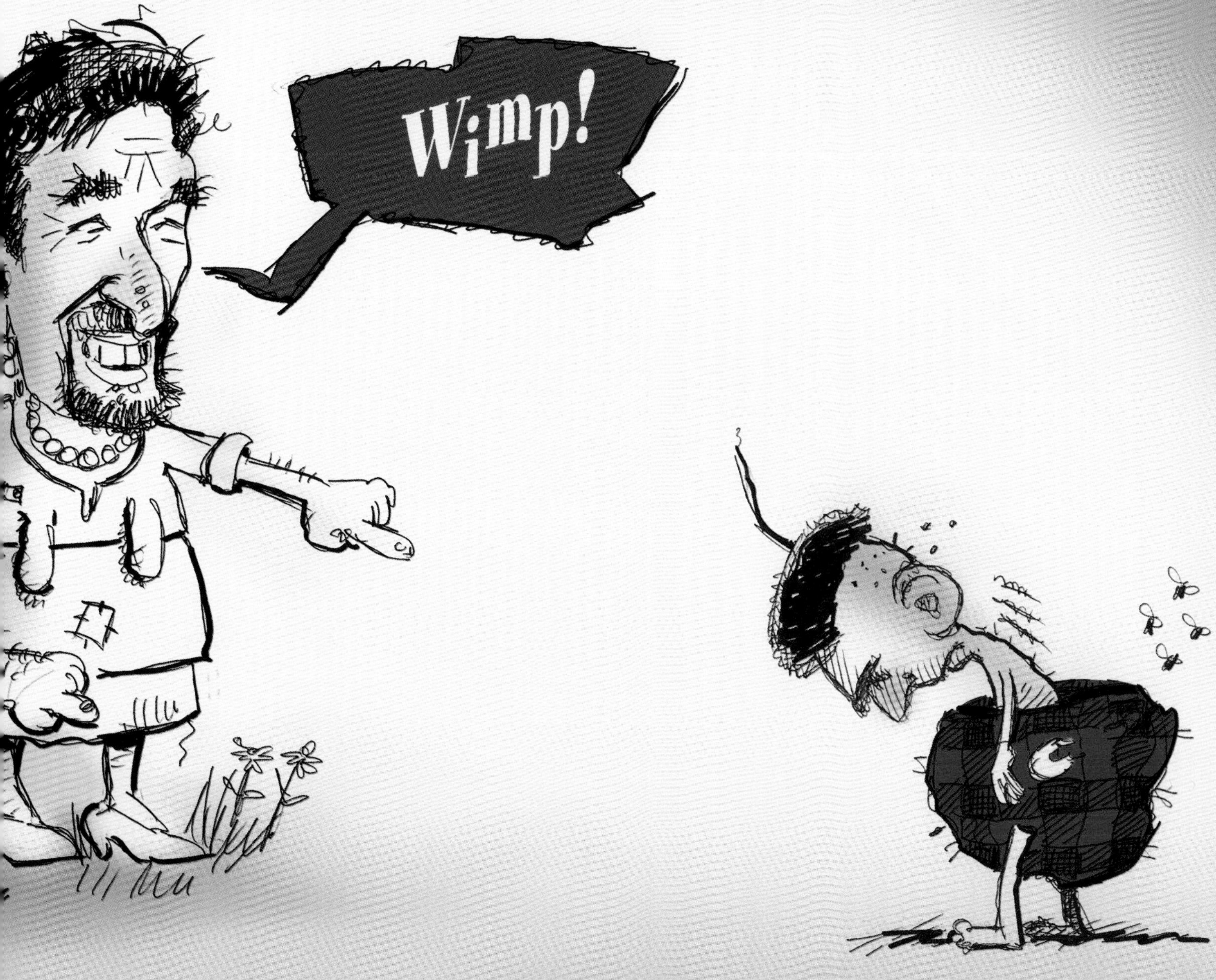
Wimp!

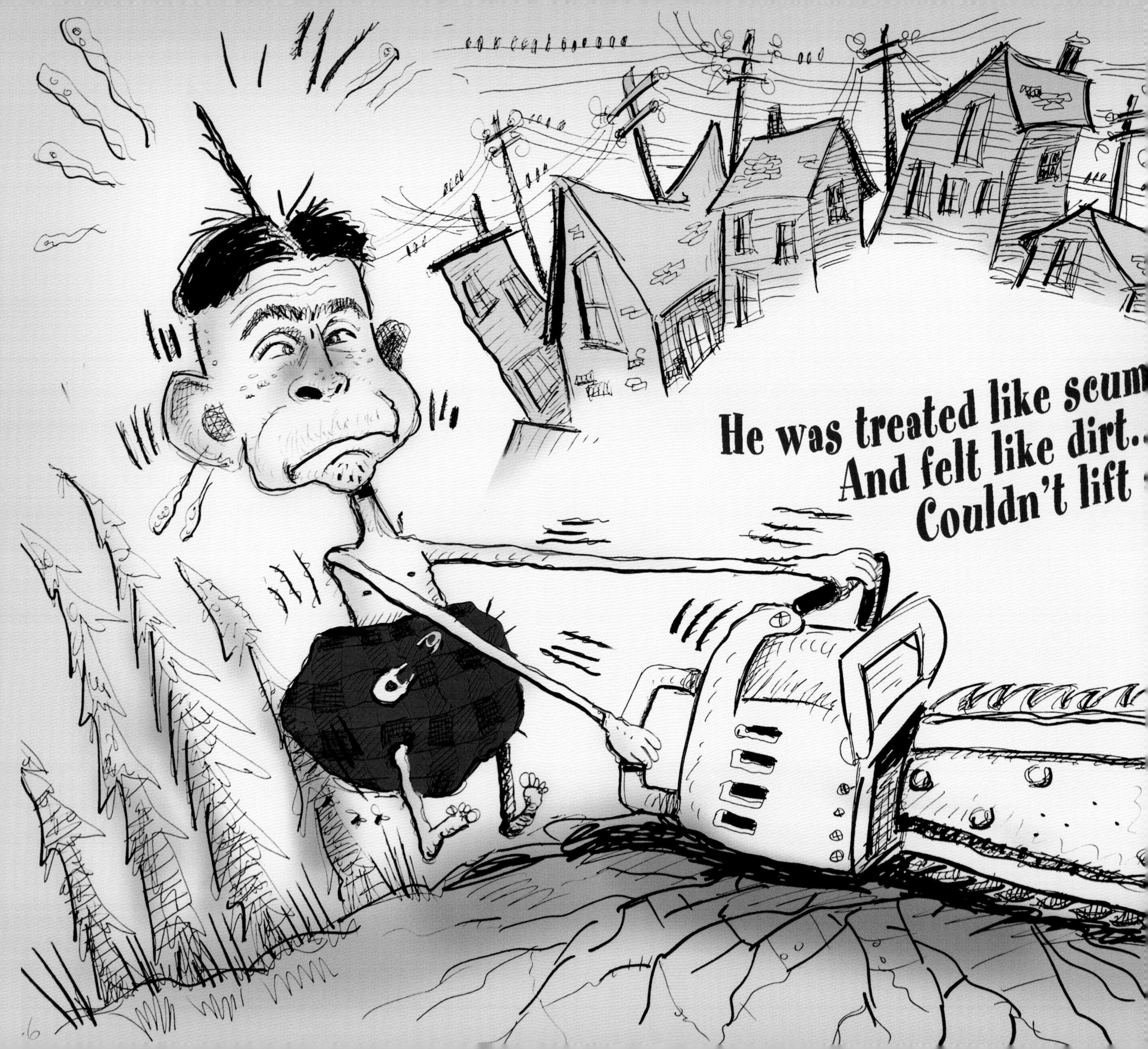

He was treated like scum
And felt like dirt...
Couldn't lift

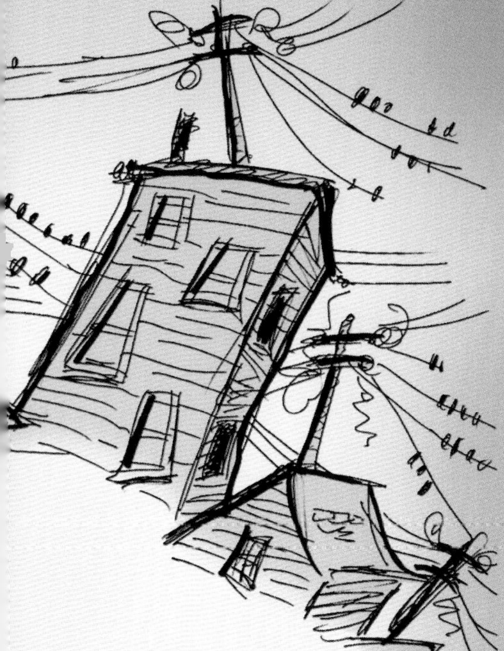

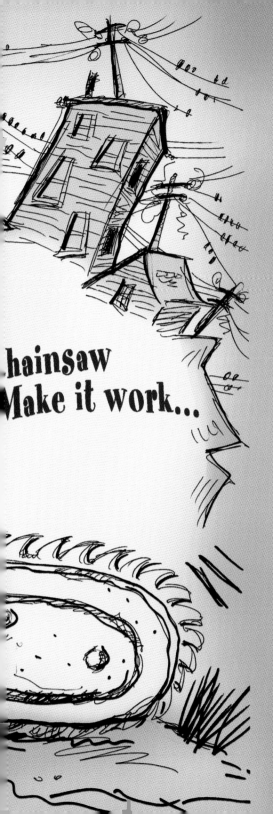

hainsaw
Make it work...

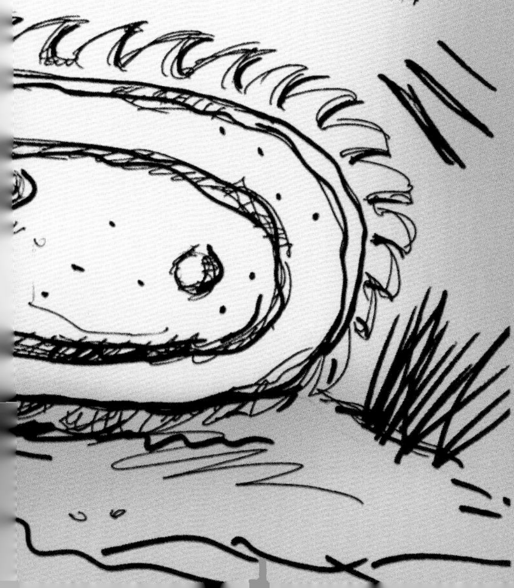

Father often said
That he didn't have a clue
Mother didn't feed him
And he hardly grew

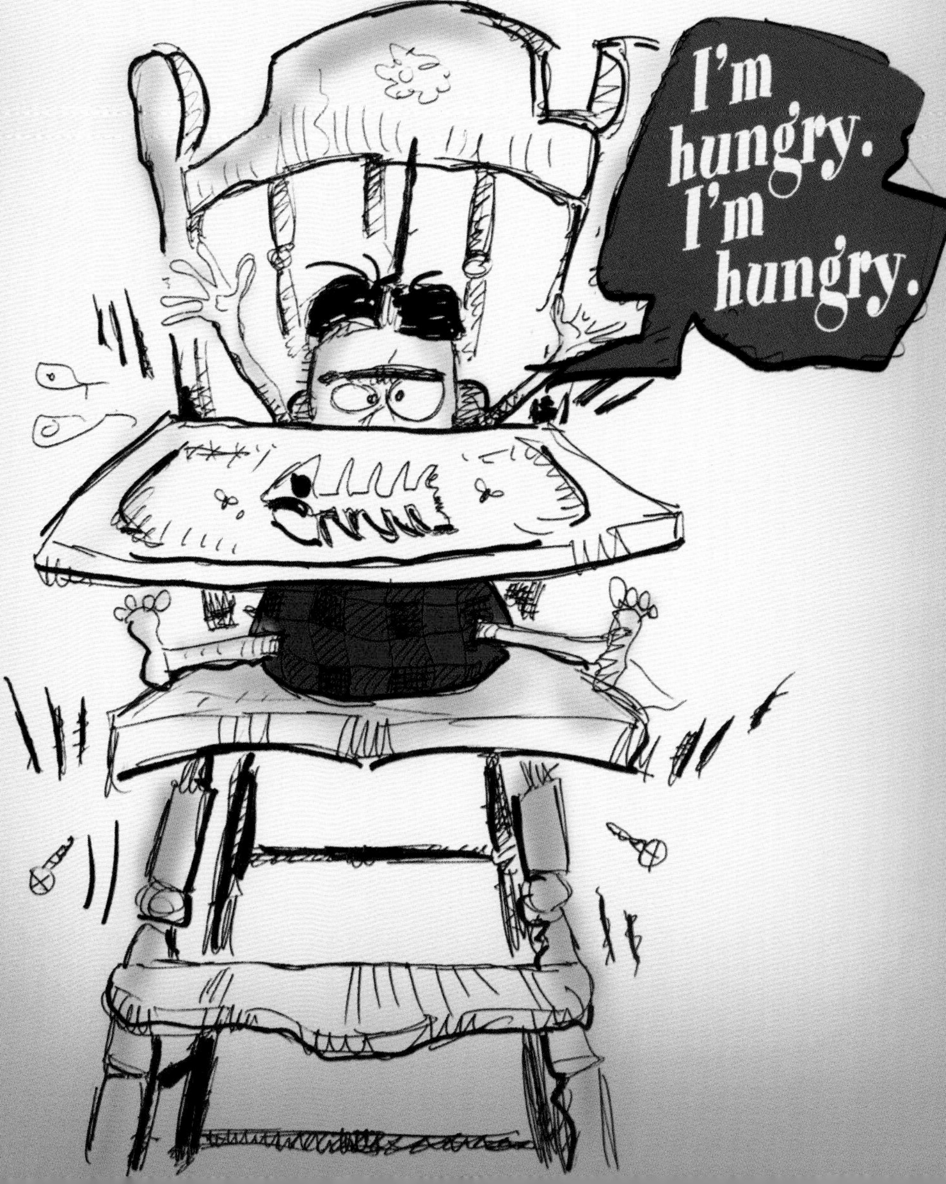
I'm hungry. I'm hungry.

Earle disappeared for fifteen years
Father didn't miss him and Mother didn't care
And after a while they forgot about Earle
And his girlfriend said...

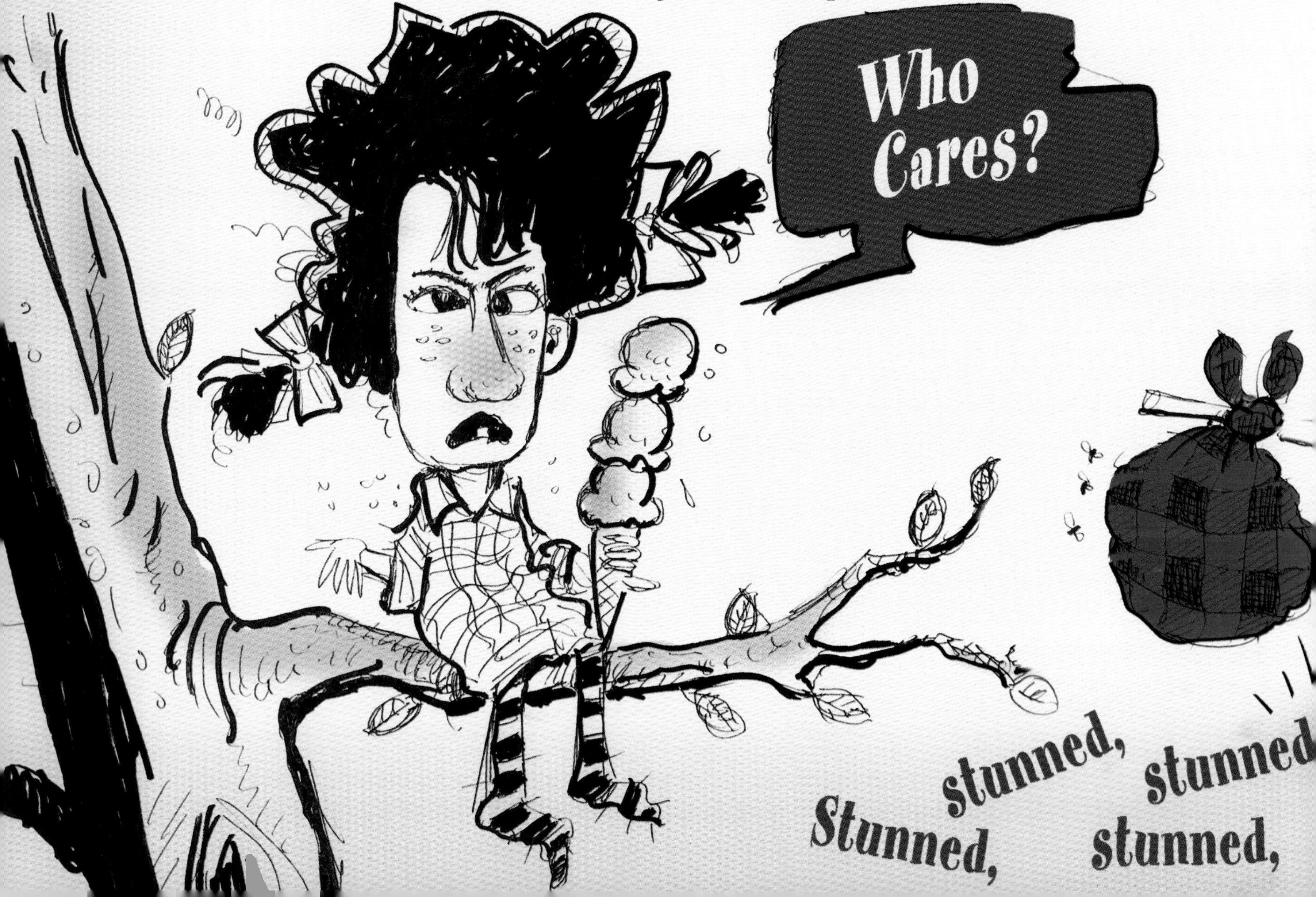
Who Cares?

Stunned, stunned, stunned, stunned,

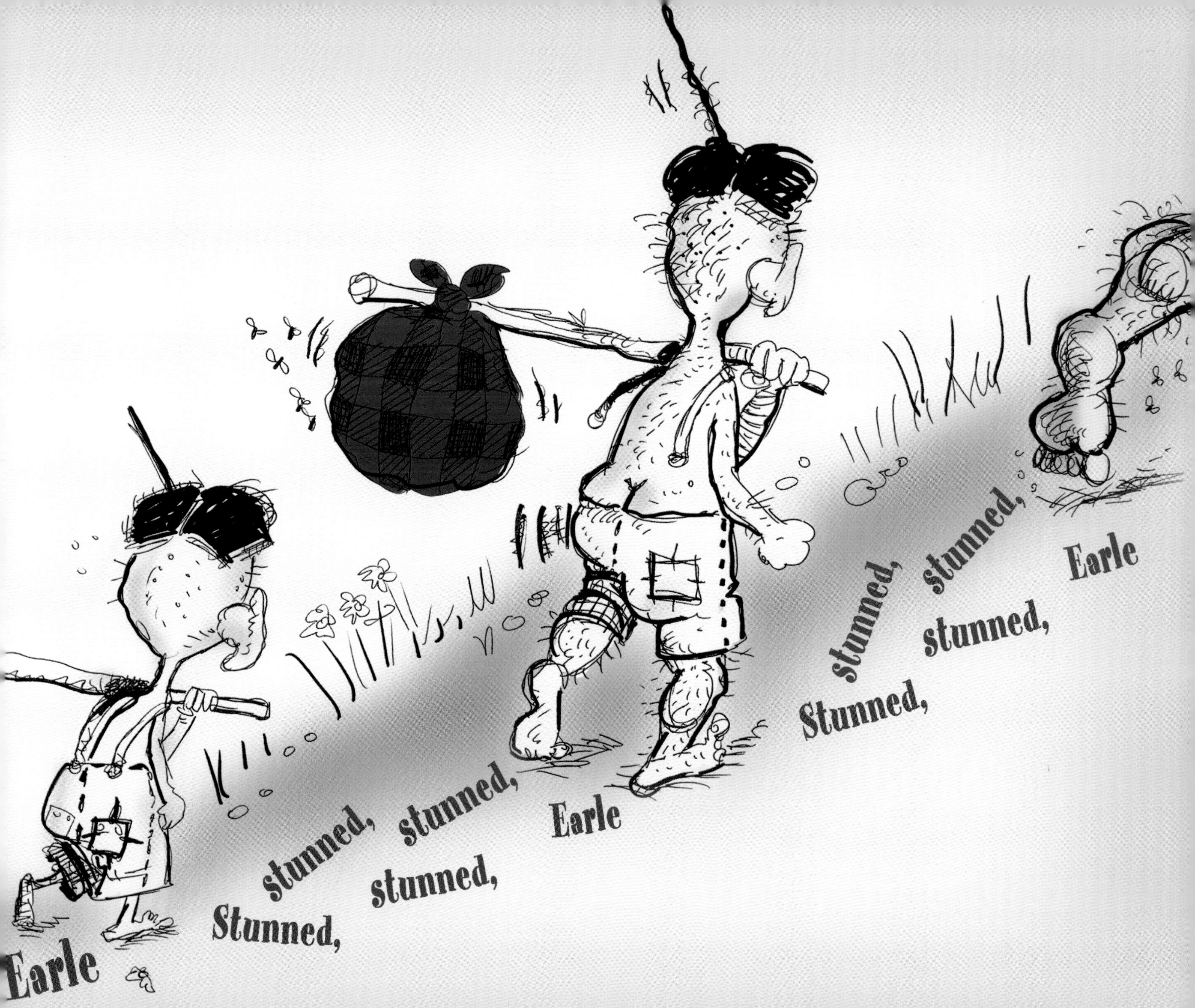

Earle

Stunned, stunned, stunned, stunned,

Earle

Stunned, stunned, stunned, stunned,

Earle

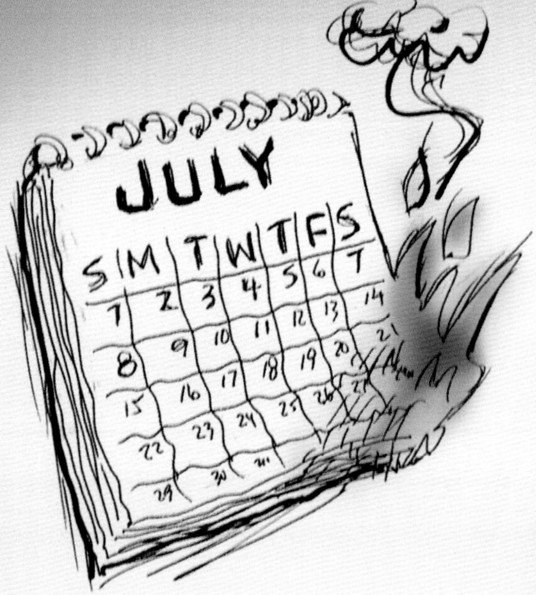
JULY
S M T W T F S

In this little town
Life went on the same
Til one hot July and
No rain came
Great big fire set the
Country ablaze
And everyone cuttin'
Fire breaks

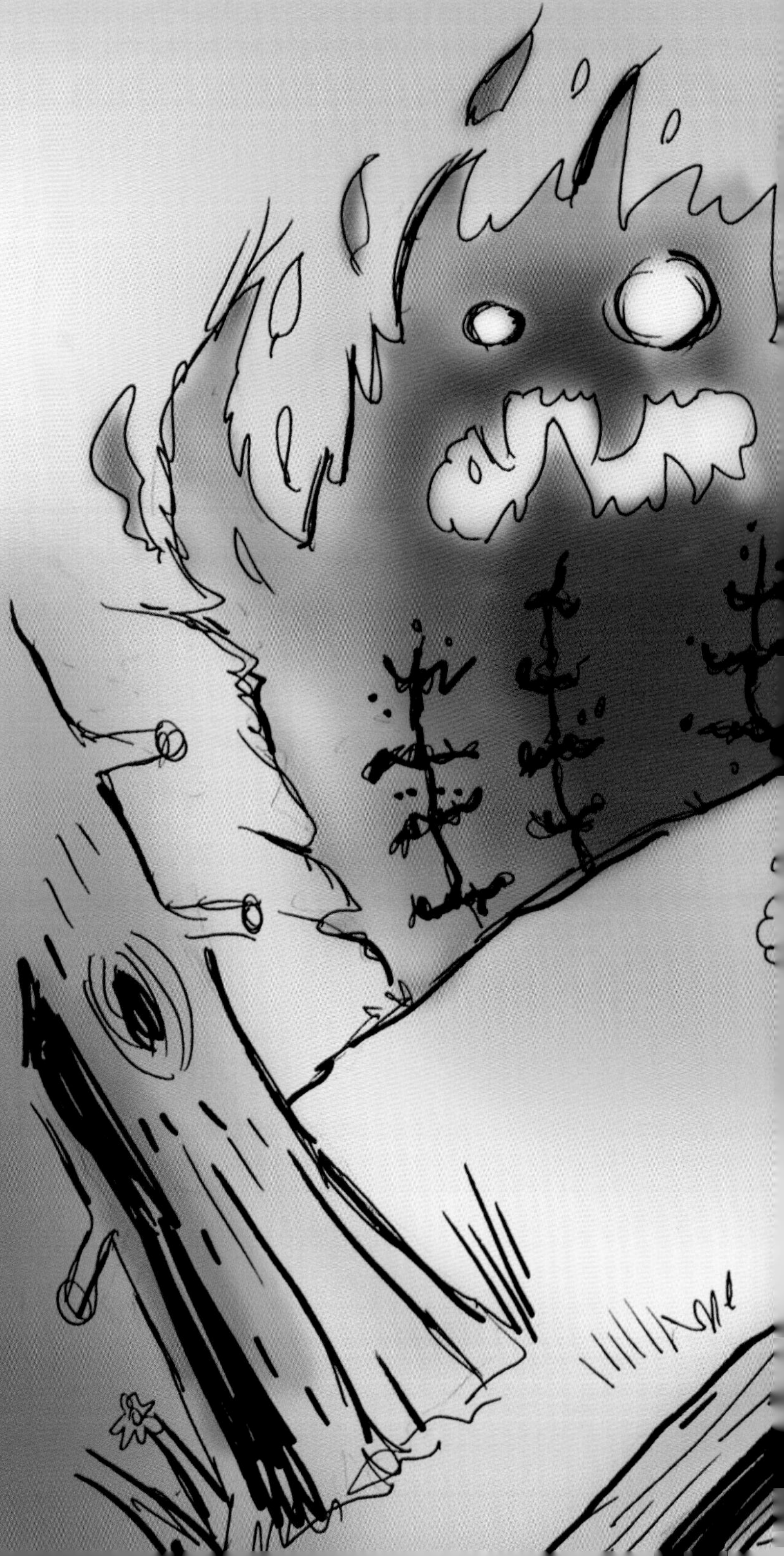

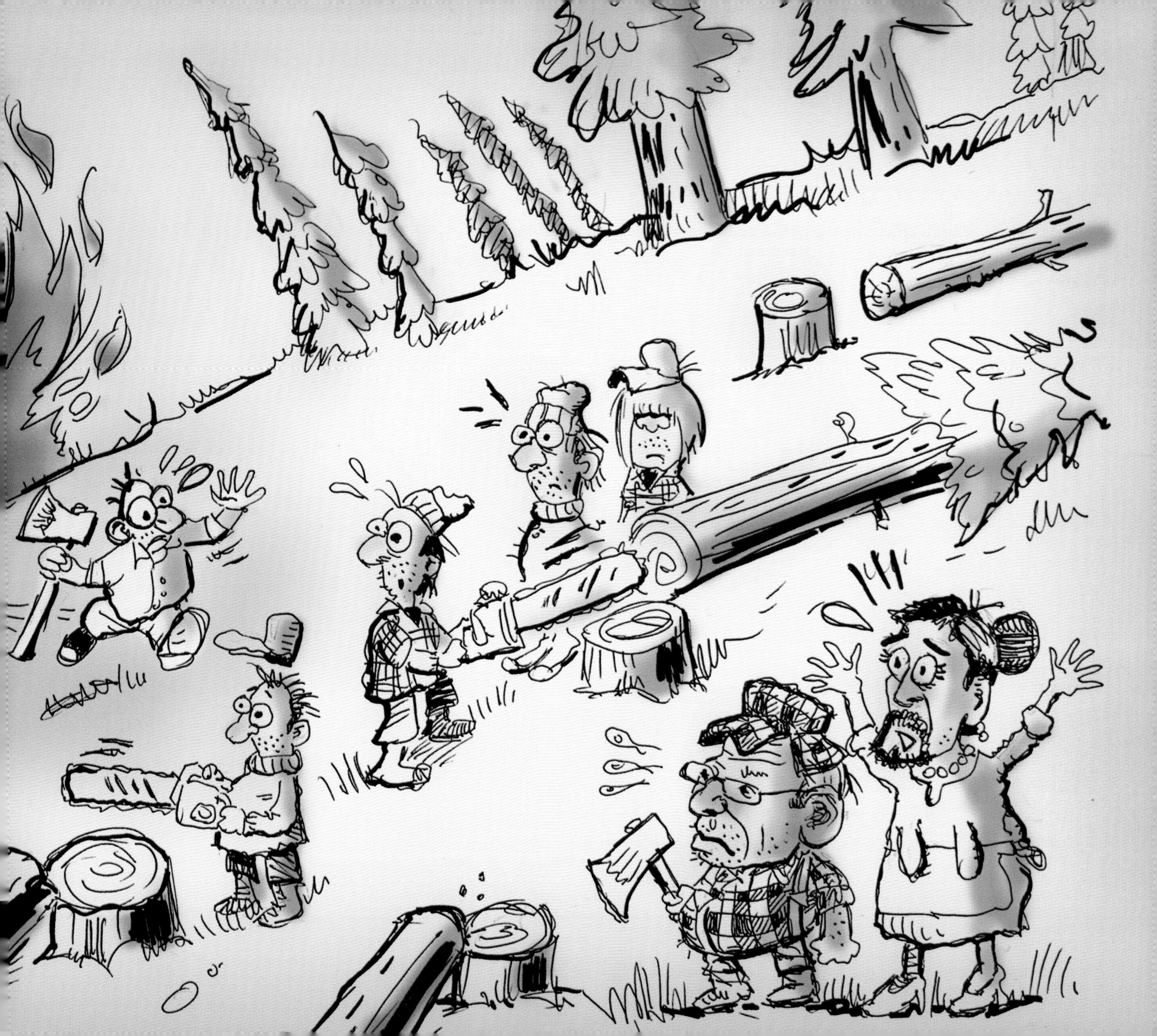

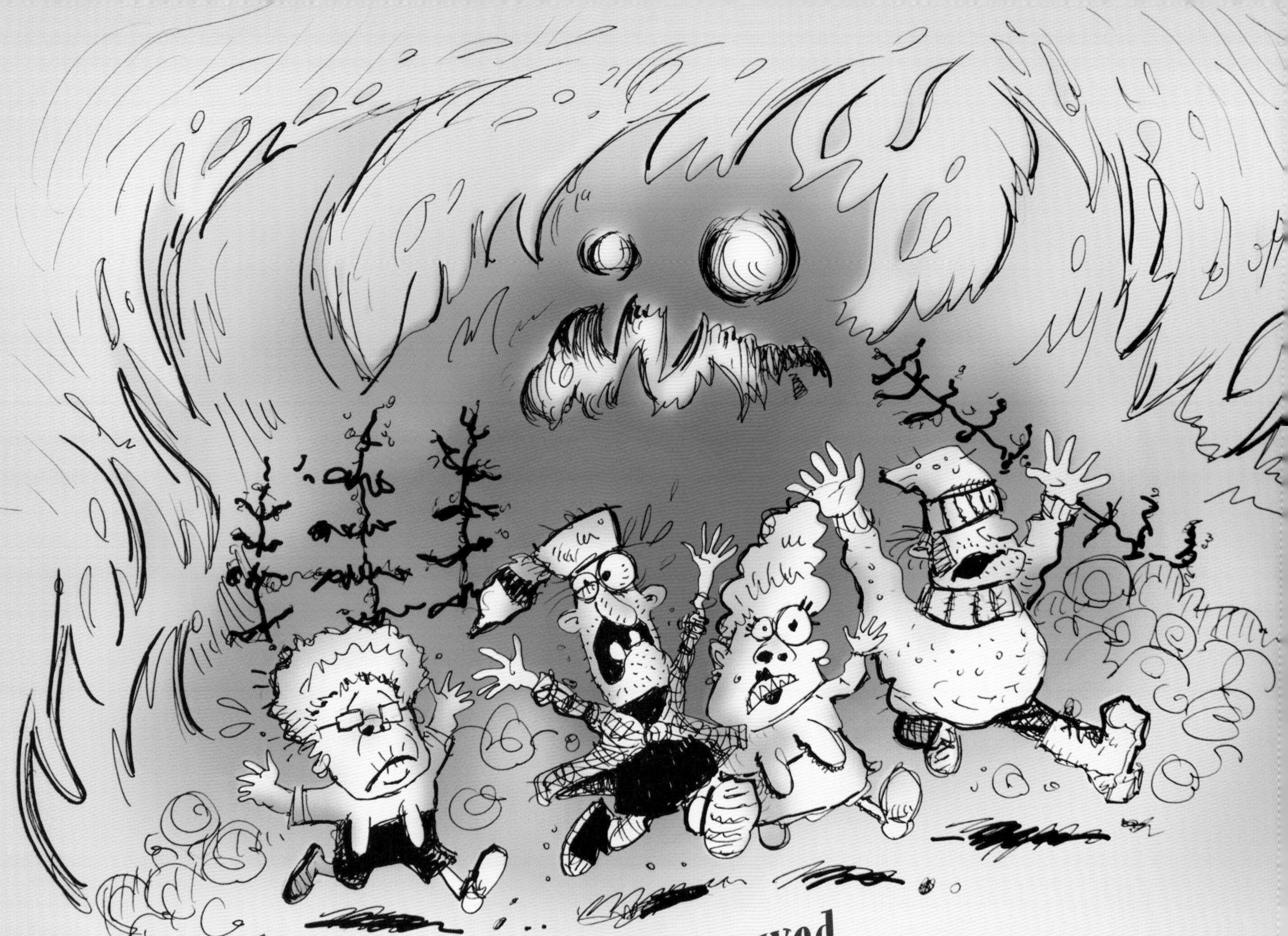

Ah they sawed and they sawed
But they couldn't outrun
The smoky fumes and fiery tongues

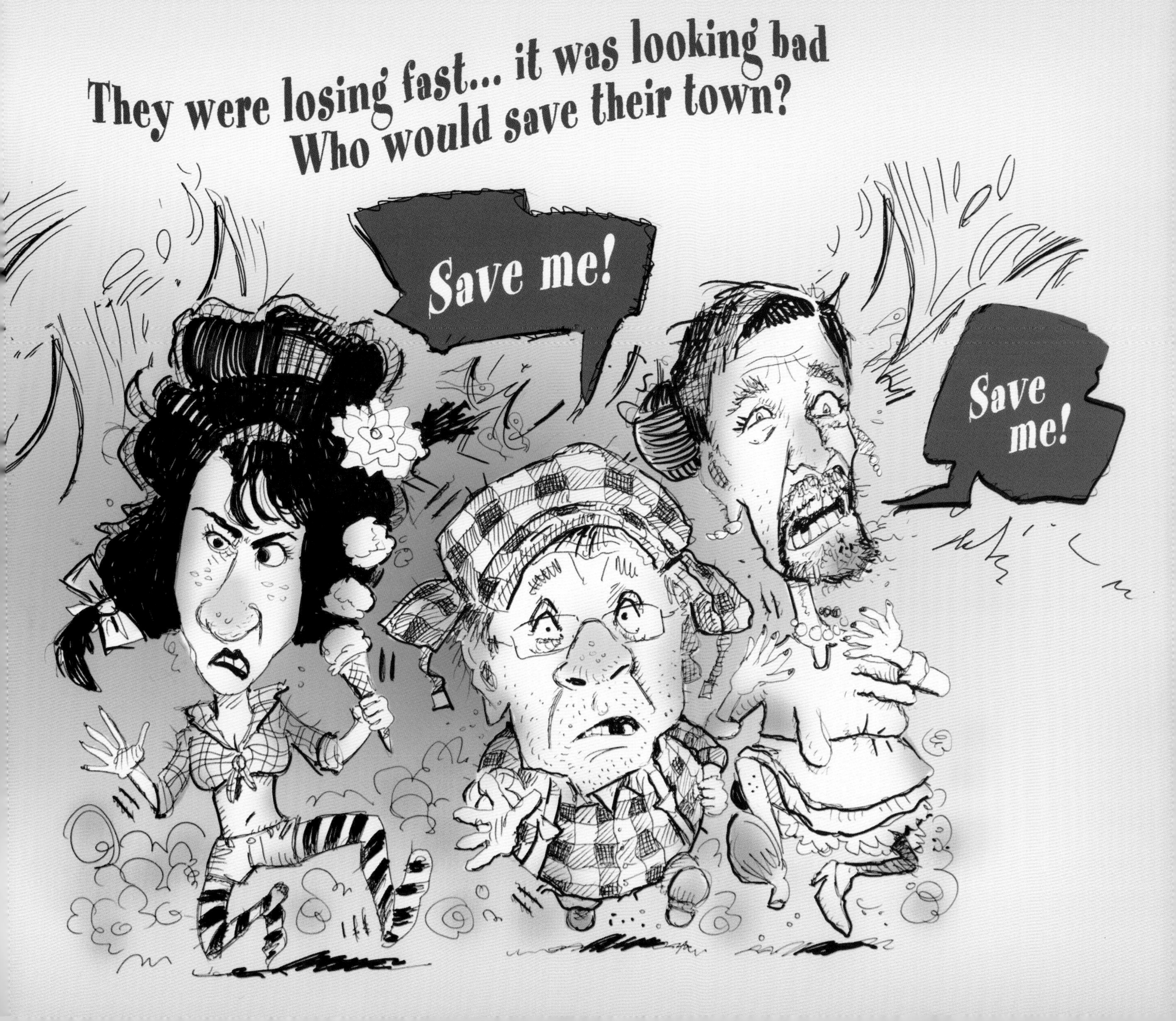
They were losing fast... it was looking bad
Who would save their town?
Save me!
Save me!

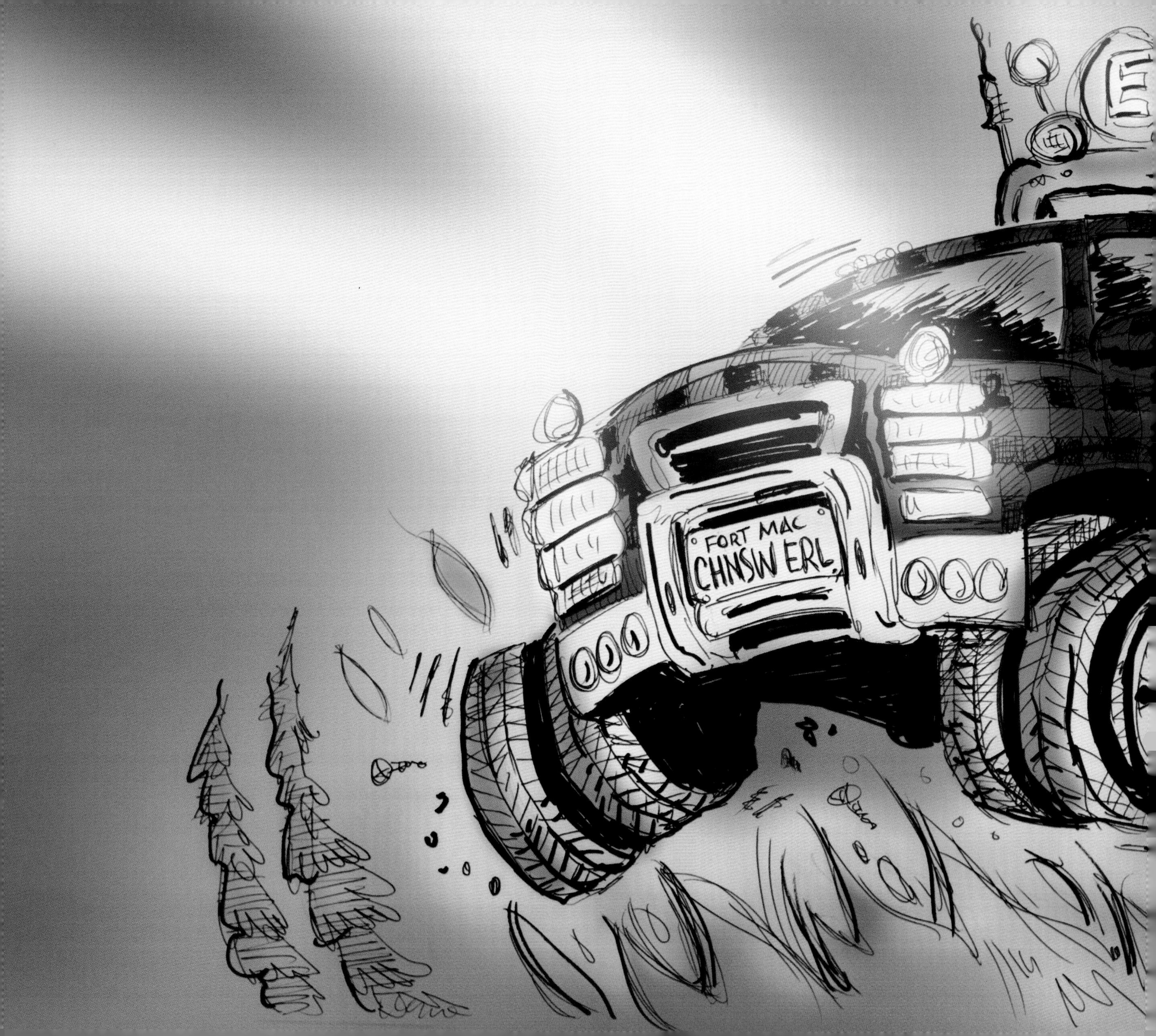
FORT MAC
CHNSW ERL

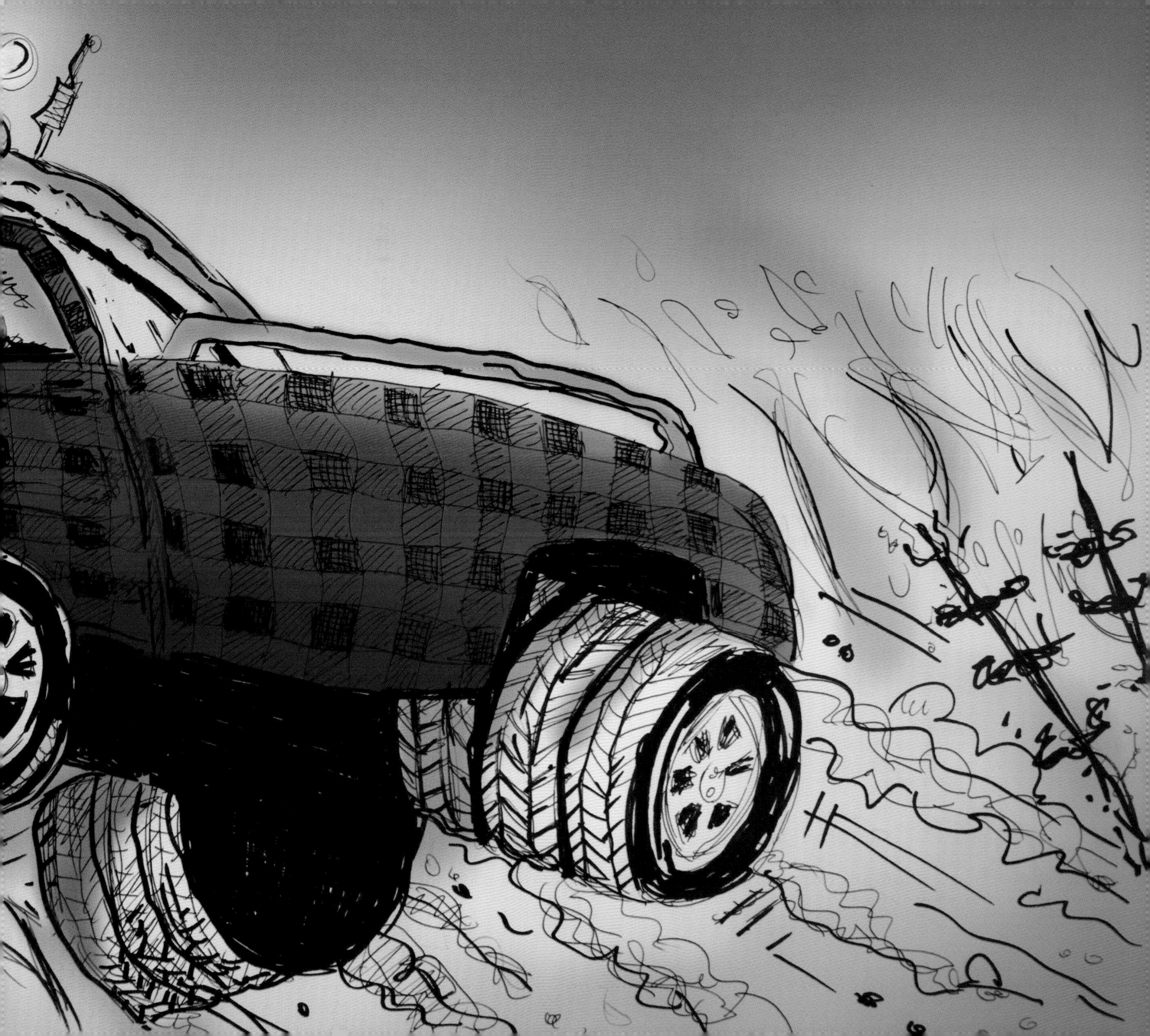

And nobody knew neither foe nor friend
That Earle had grown to seven foot ten

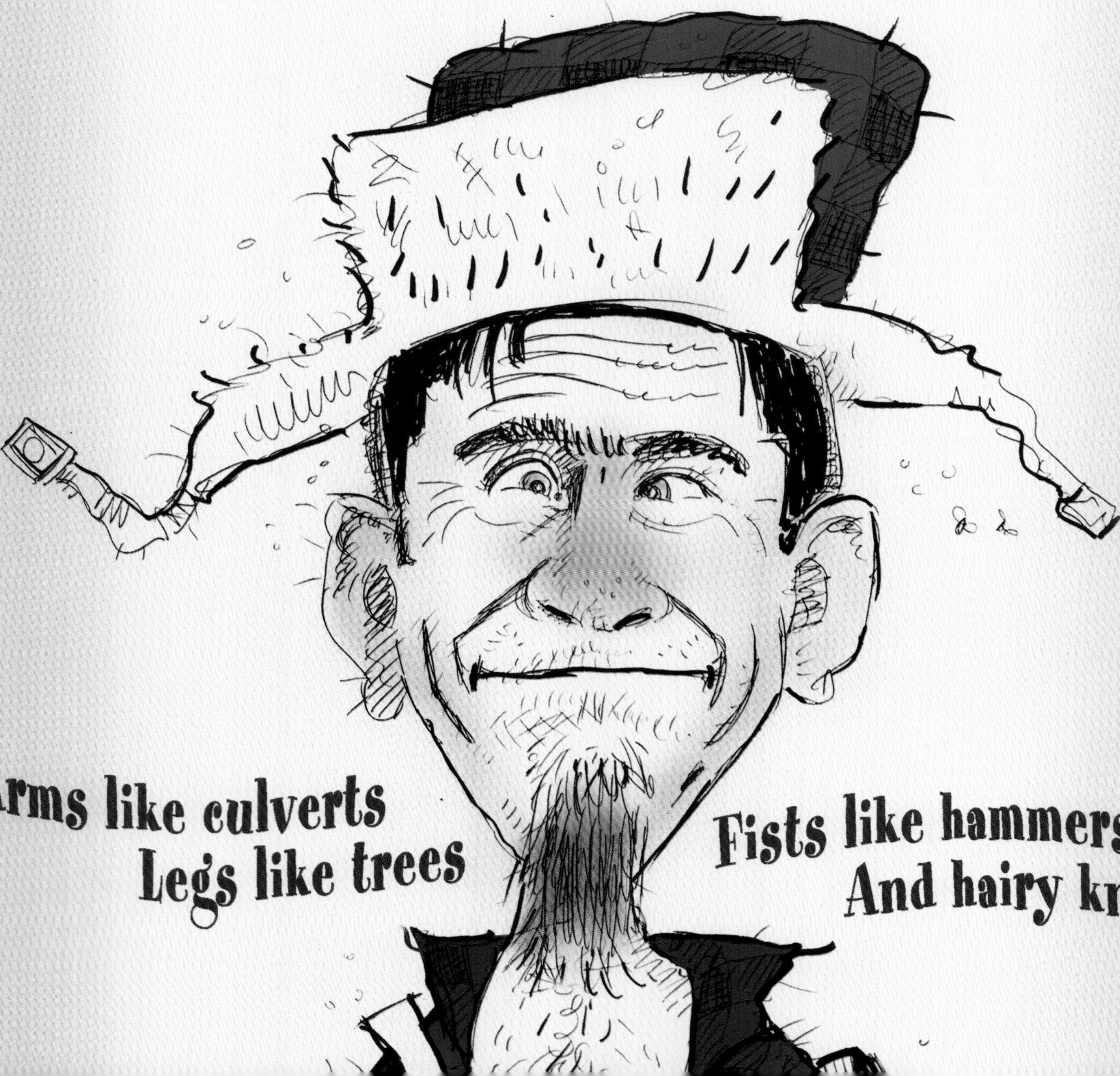

Arms like culverts
Legs like trees

Fists like hammers
And hairy knees

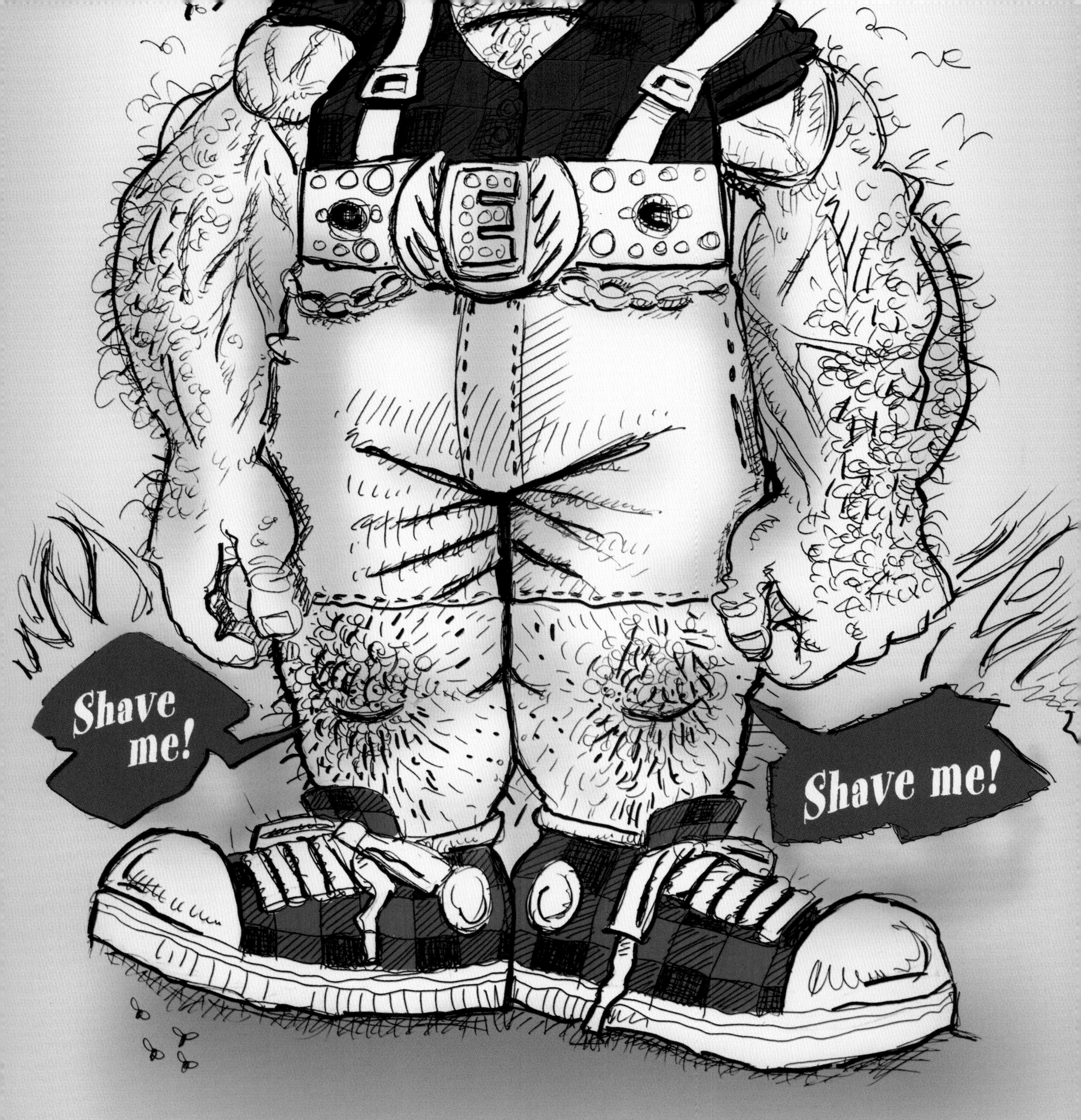
Shave me!
Shave me!

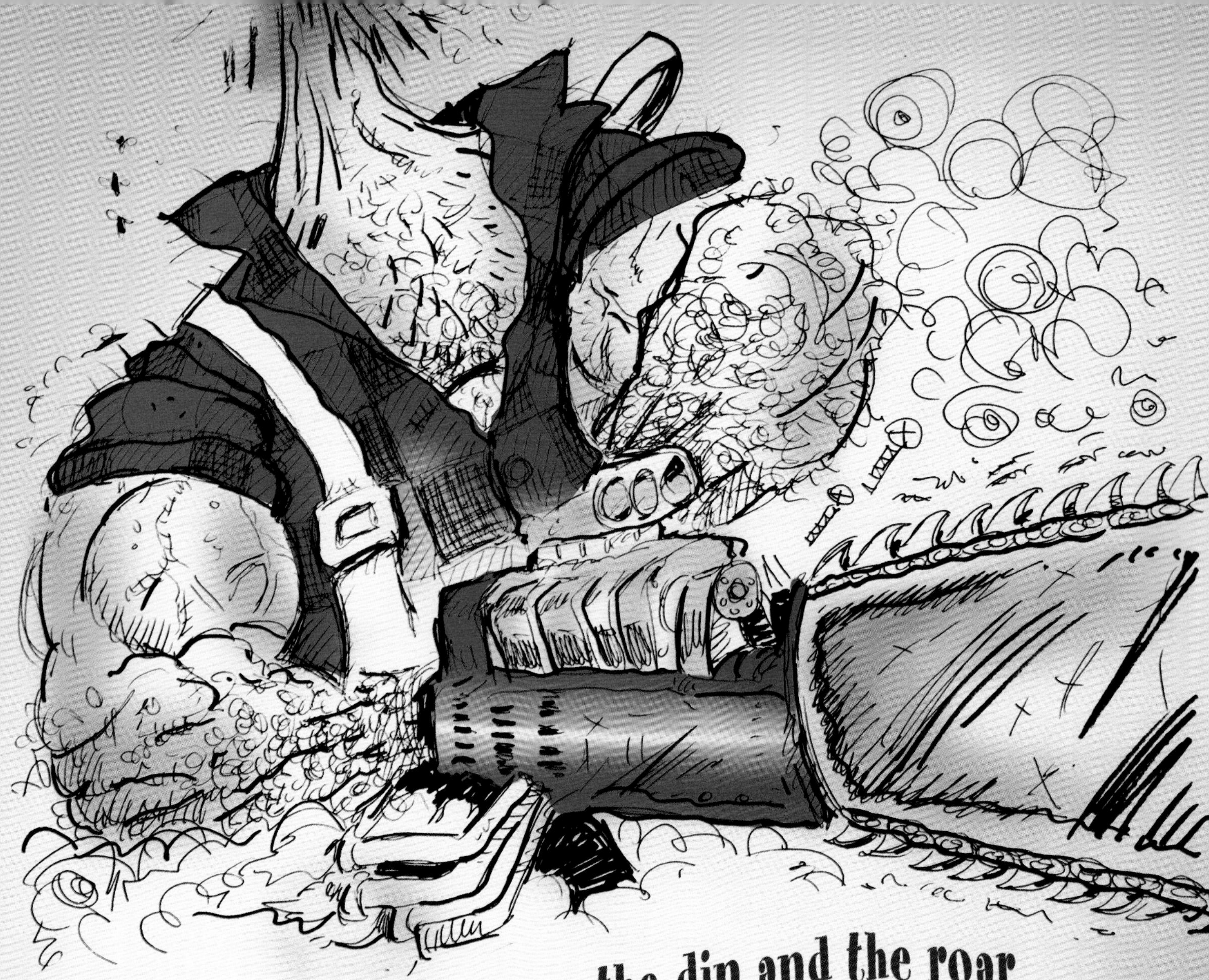

Far off in the woods above the din and the roar
Came a sound nobody had heard before
Trees were fallin' like a tidal wave to a
Monster Jonsered chainsaw

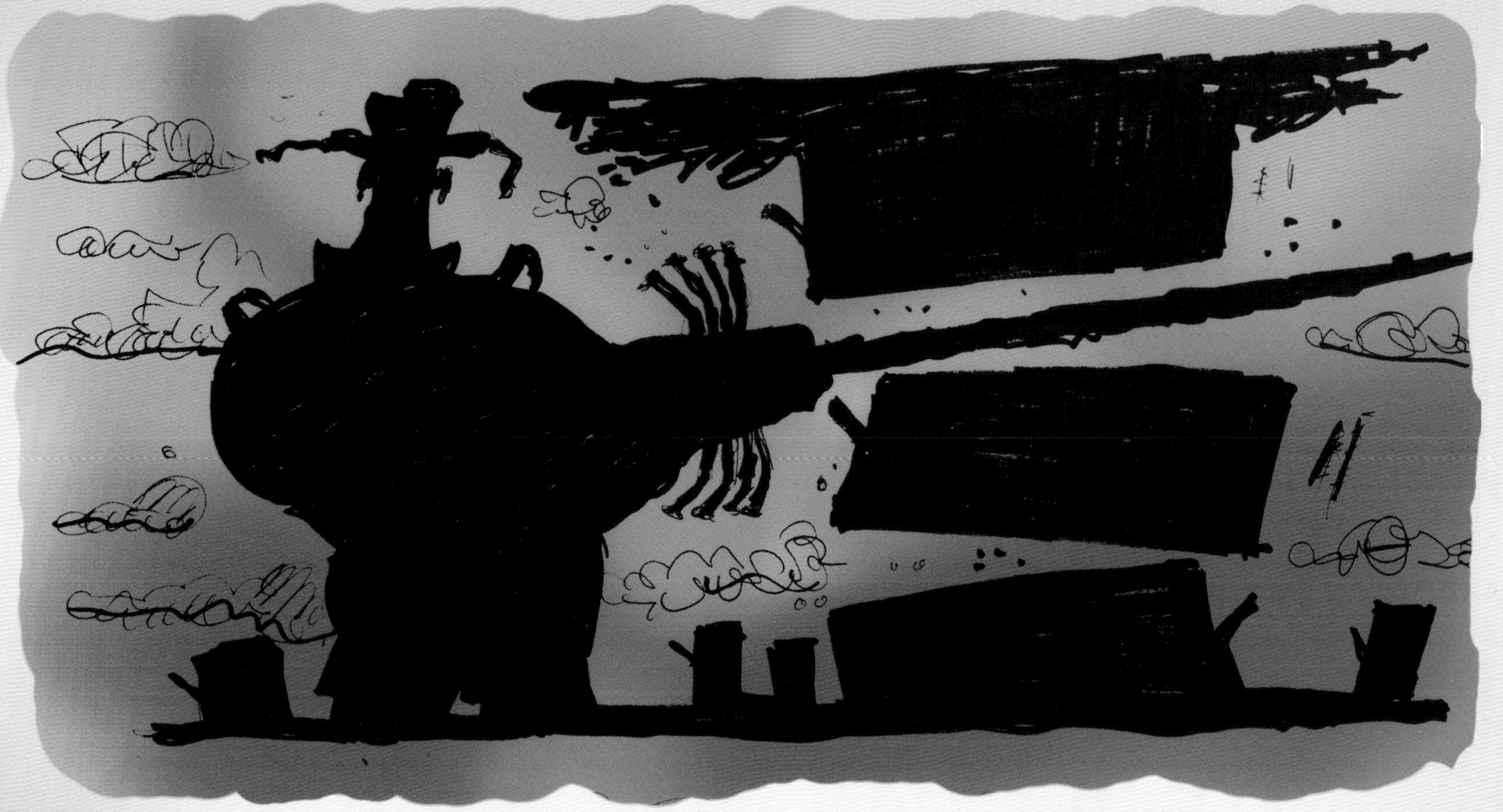

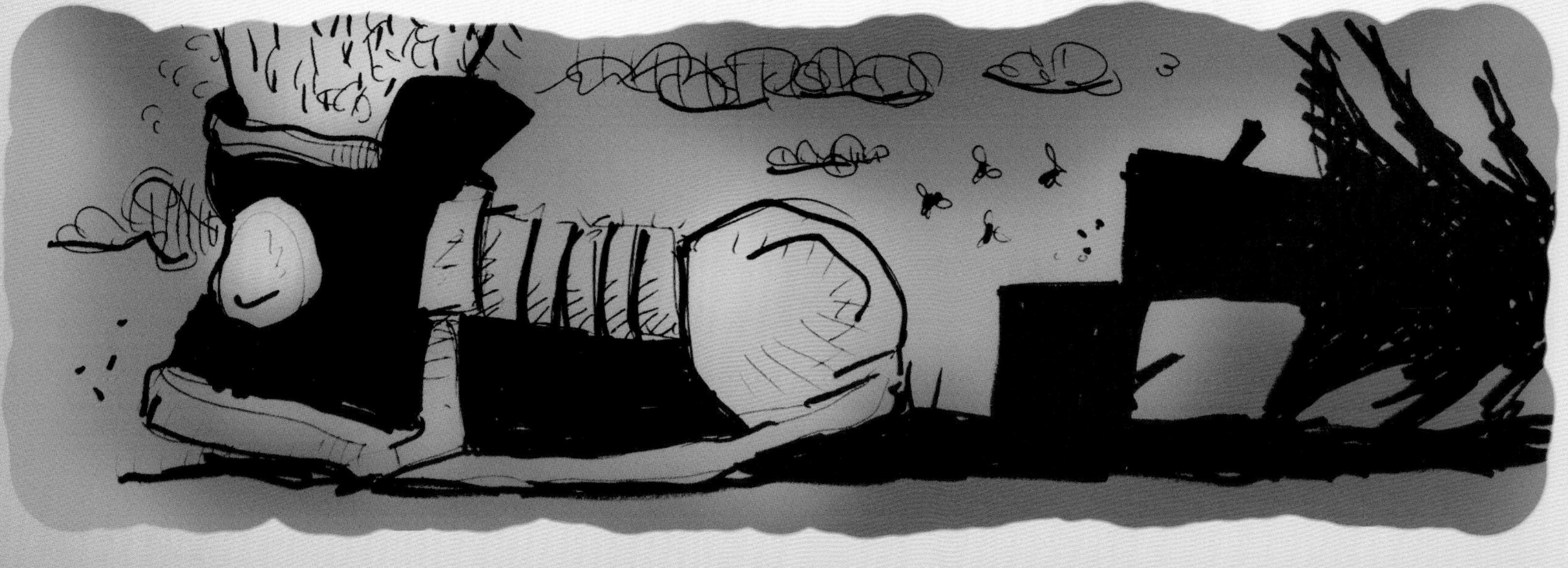

Chain,
Chain,
Chainsaw Earle,

Chain, Chain,
Chainsaw Earle,

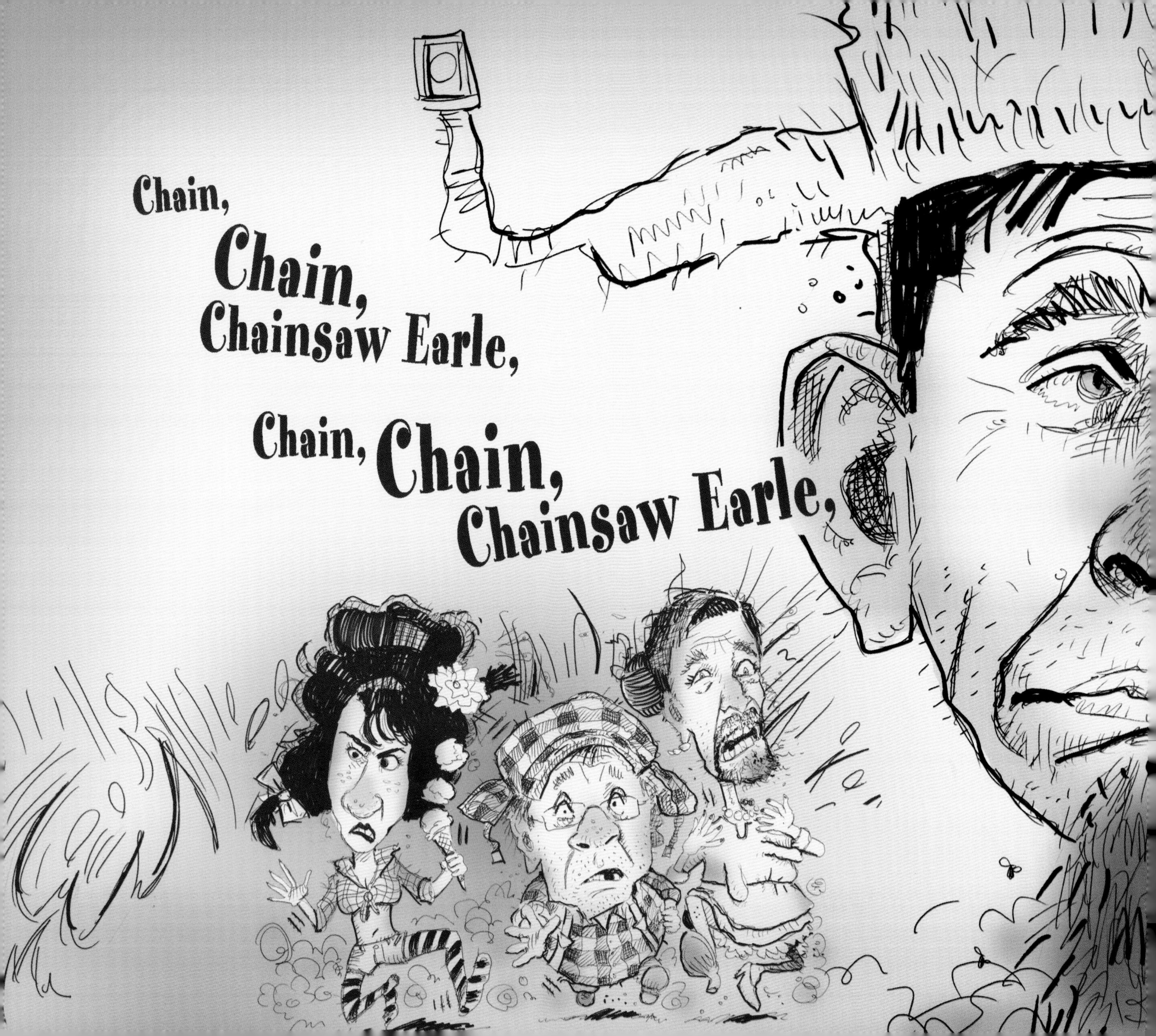

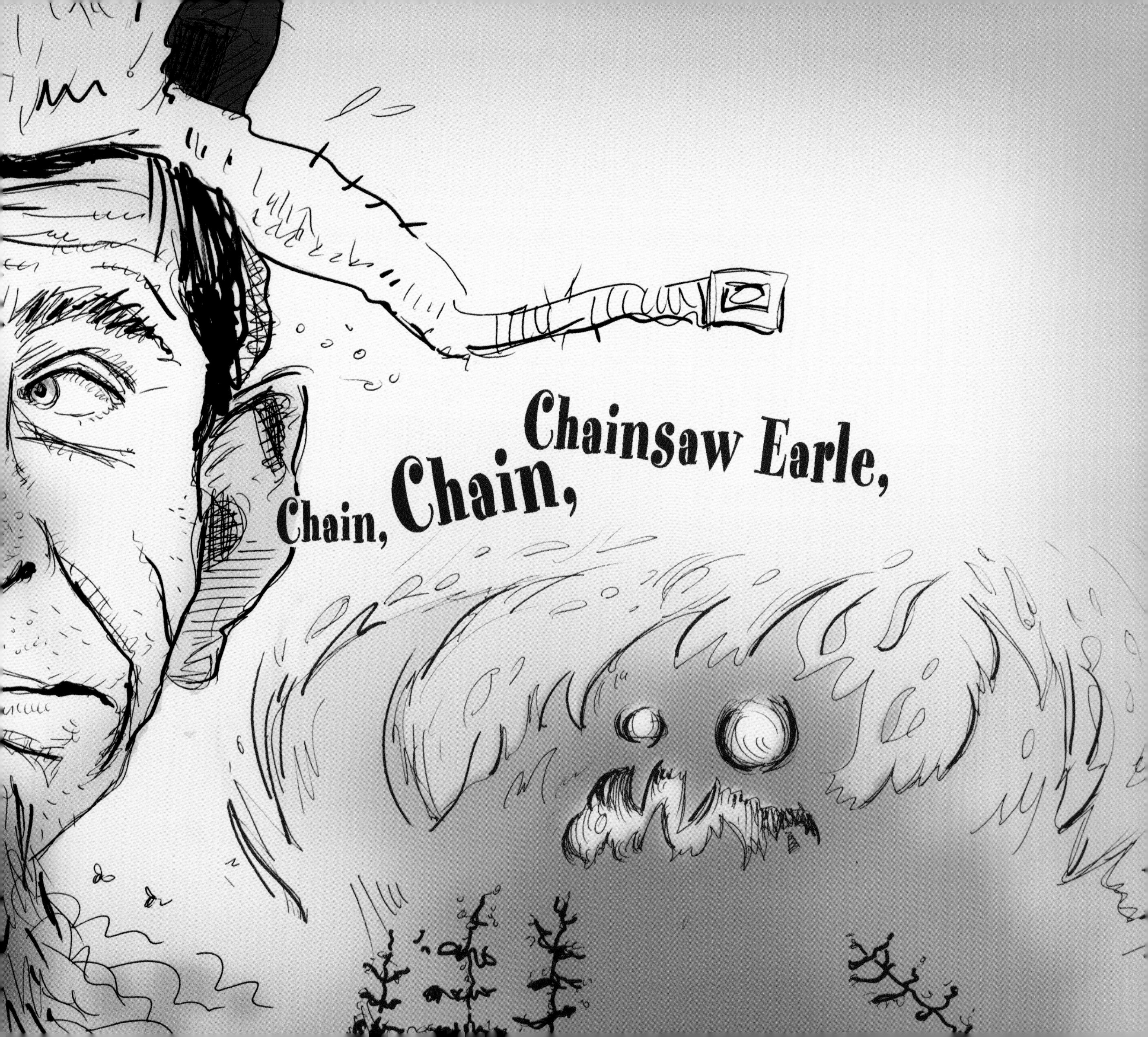

Chain, Chain, Chainsaw Earle,

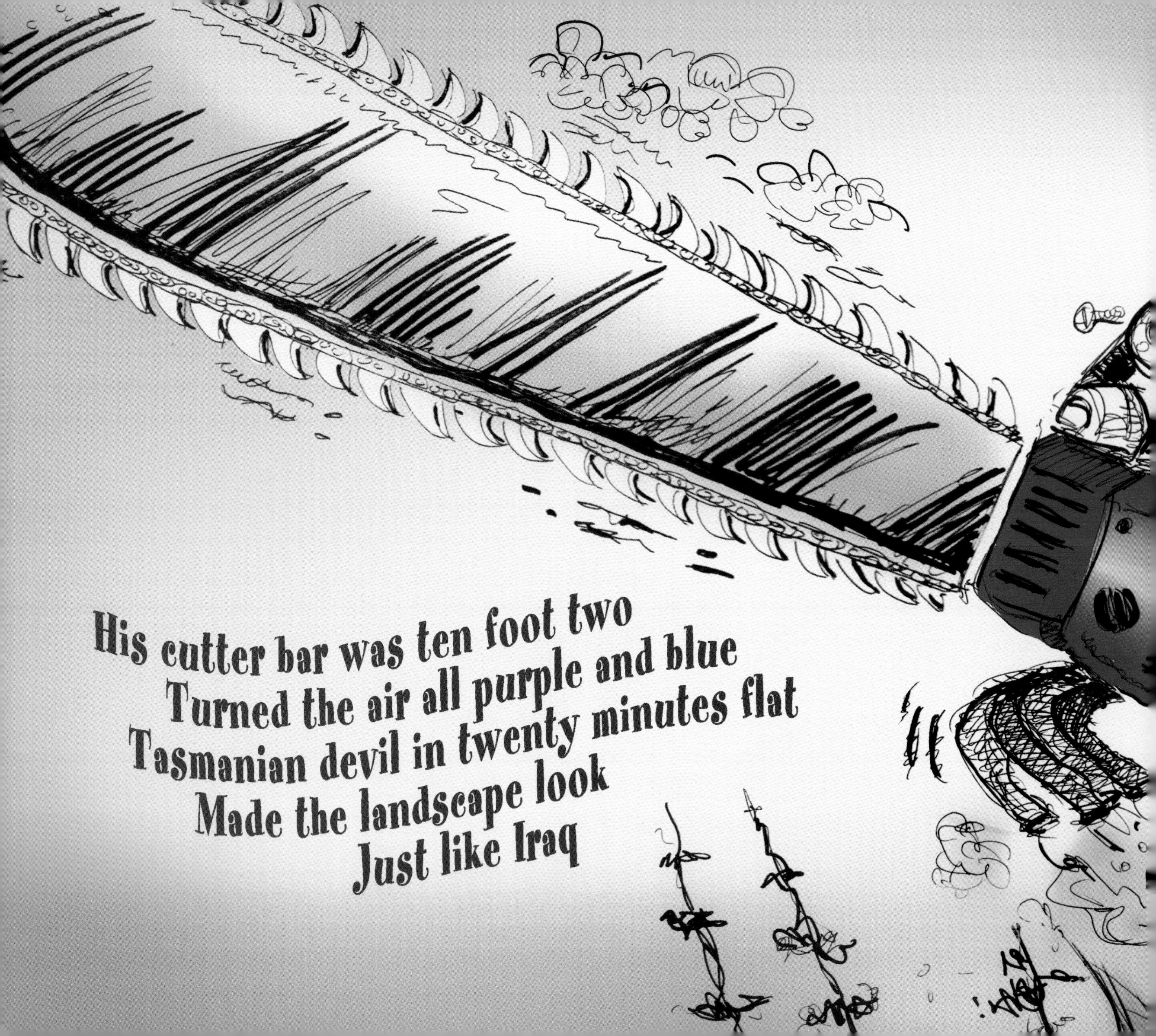

His cutter bar was ten foot two
Turned the air all purple and blue
Tasmanian devil in twenty minutes flat
Made the landscape look
Just like Iraq

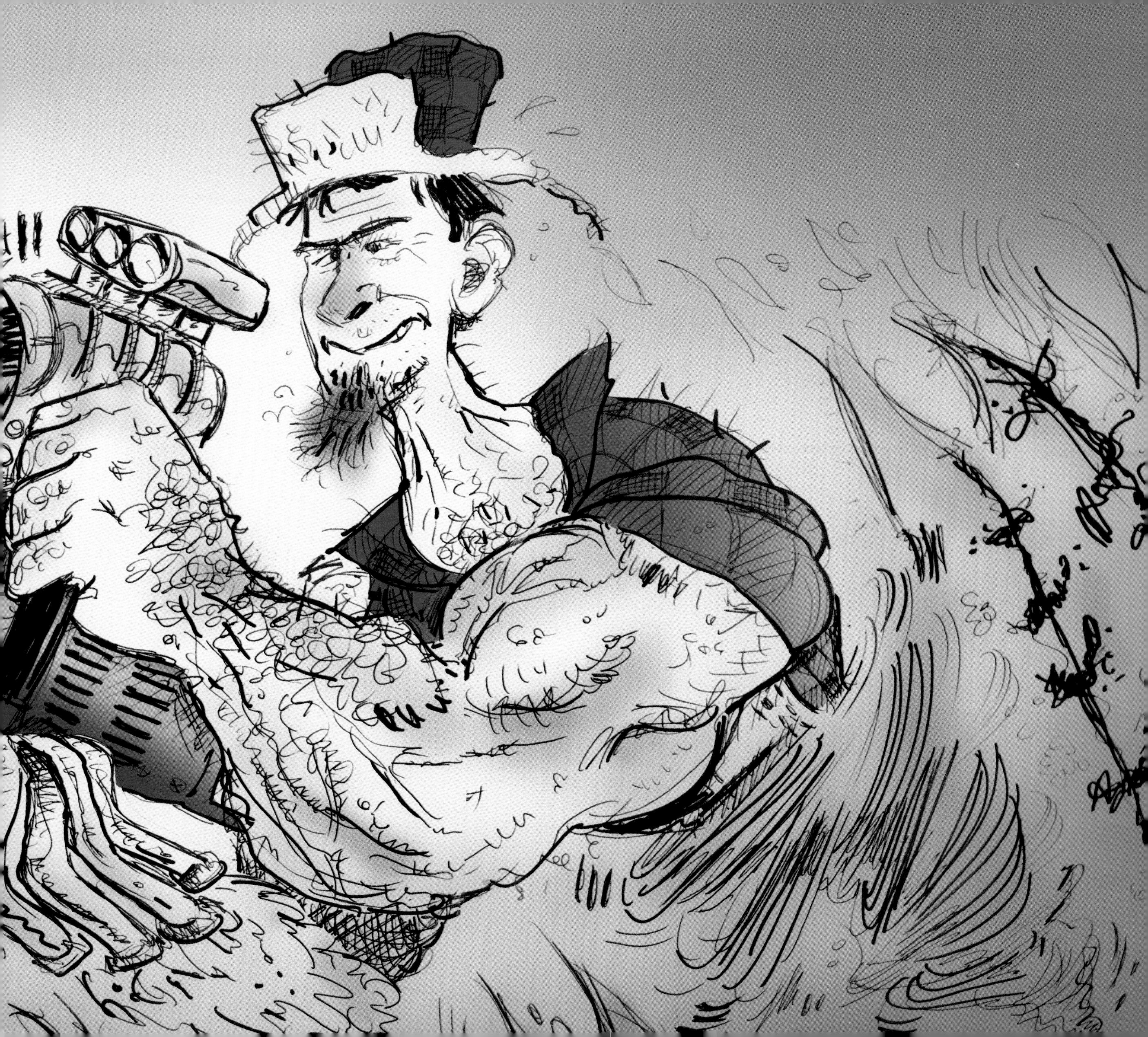

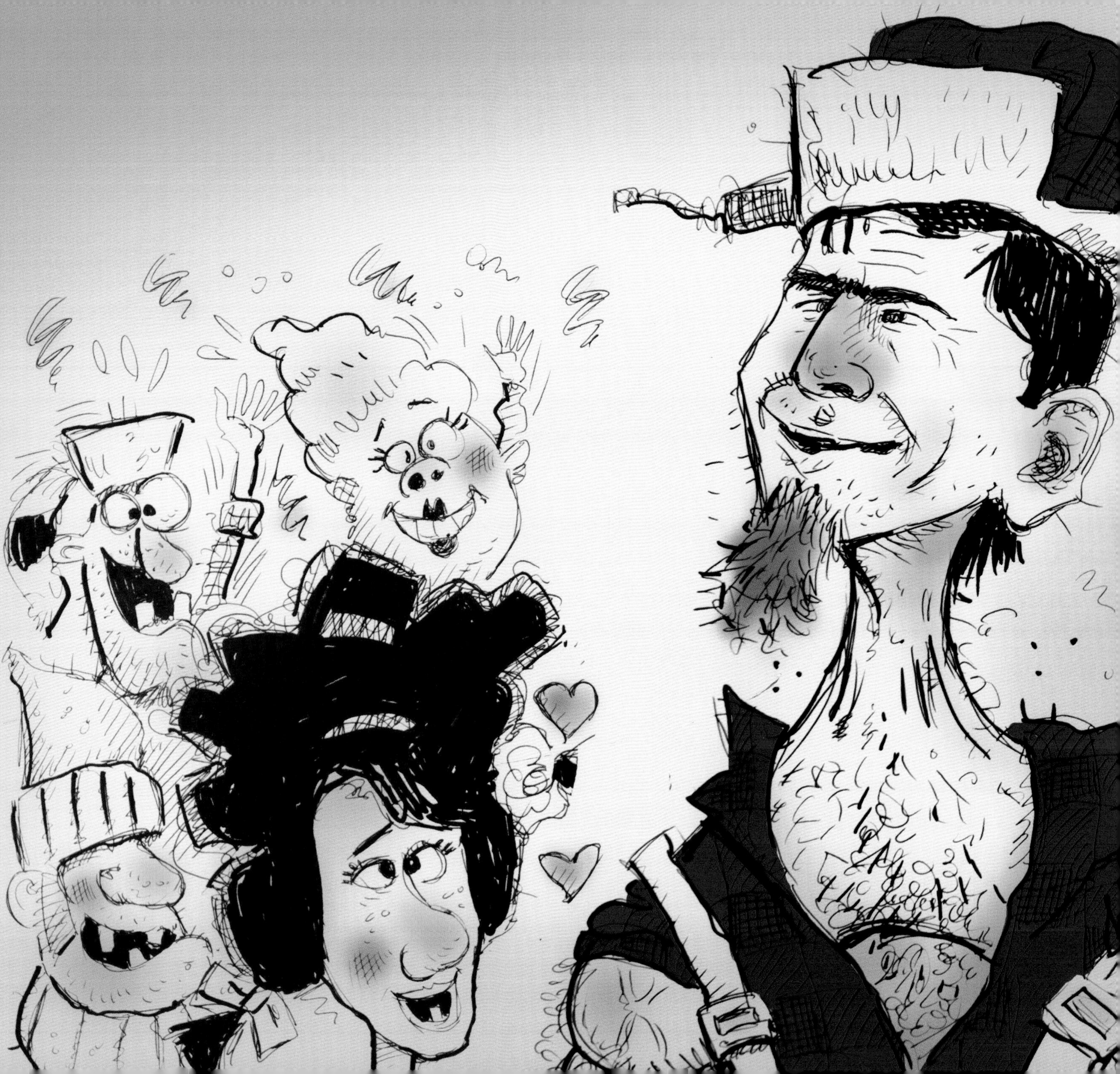

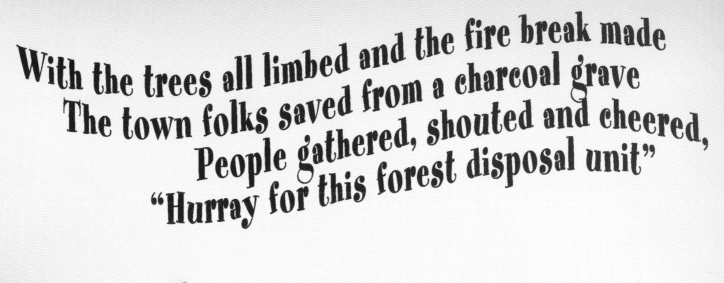

With the trees all limbed and the fire break made
The town folks saved from a charcoal grave
People gathered, shouted and cheered,
"Hurray for this forest disposal unit"

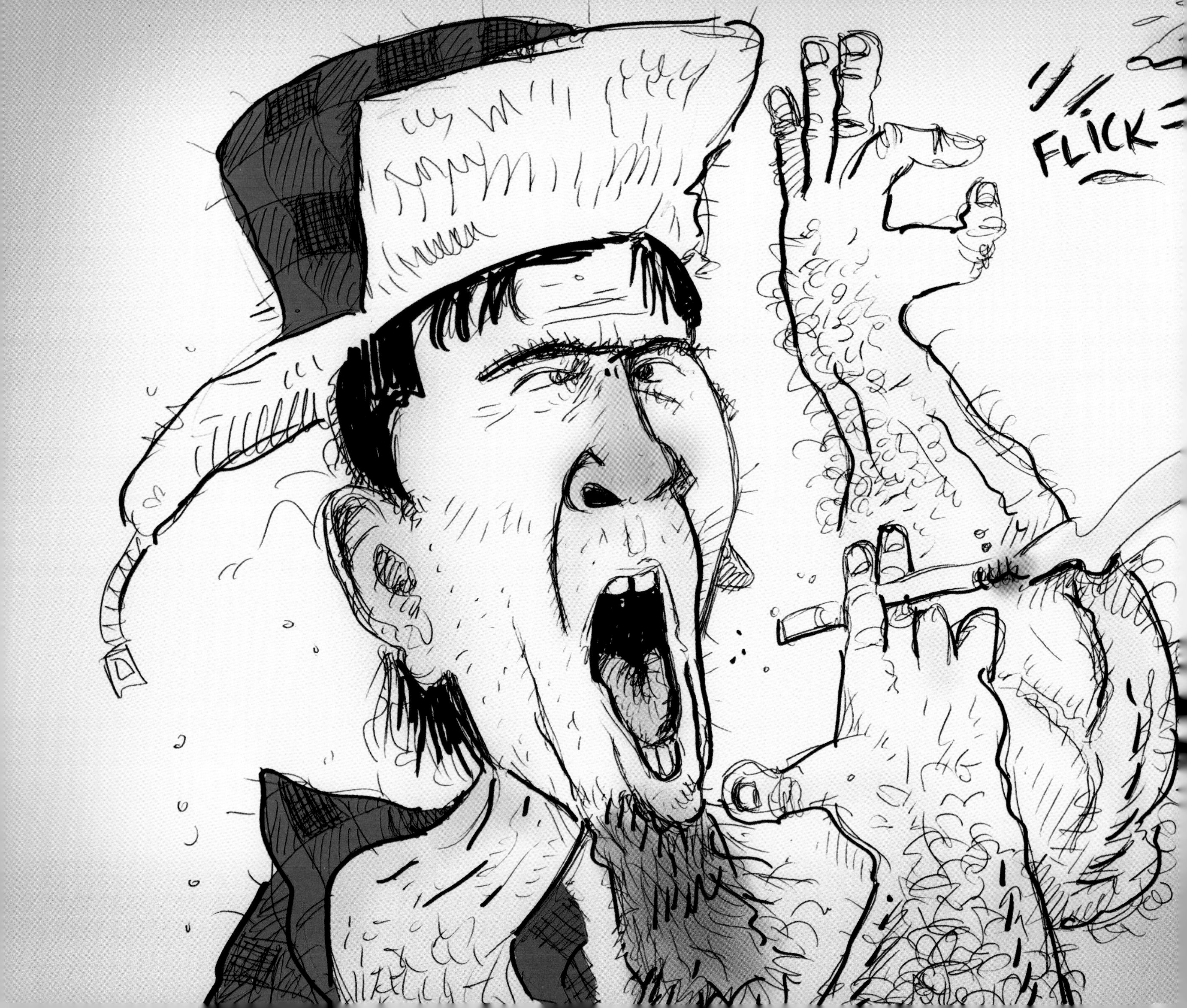
FLICK

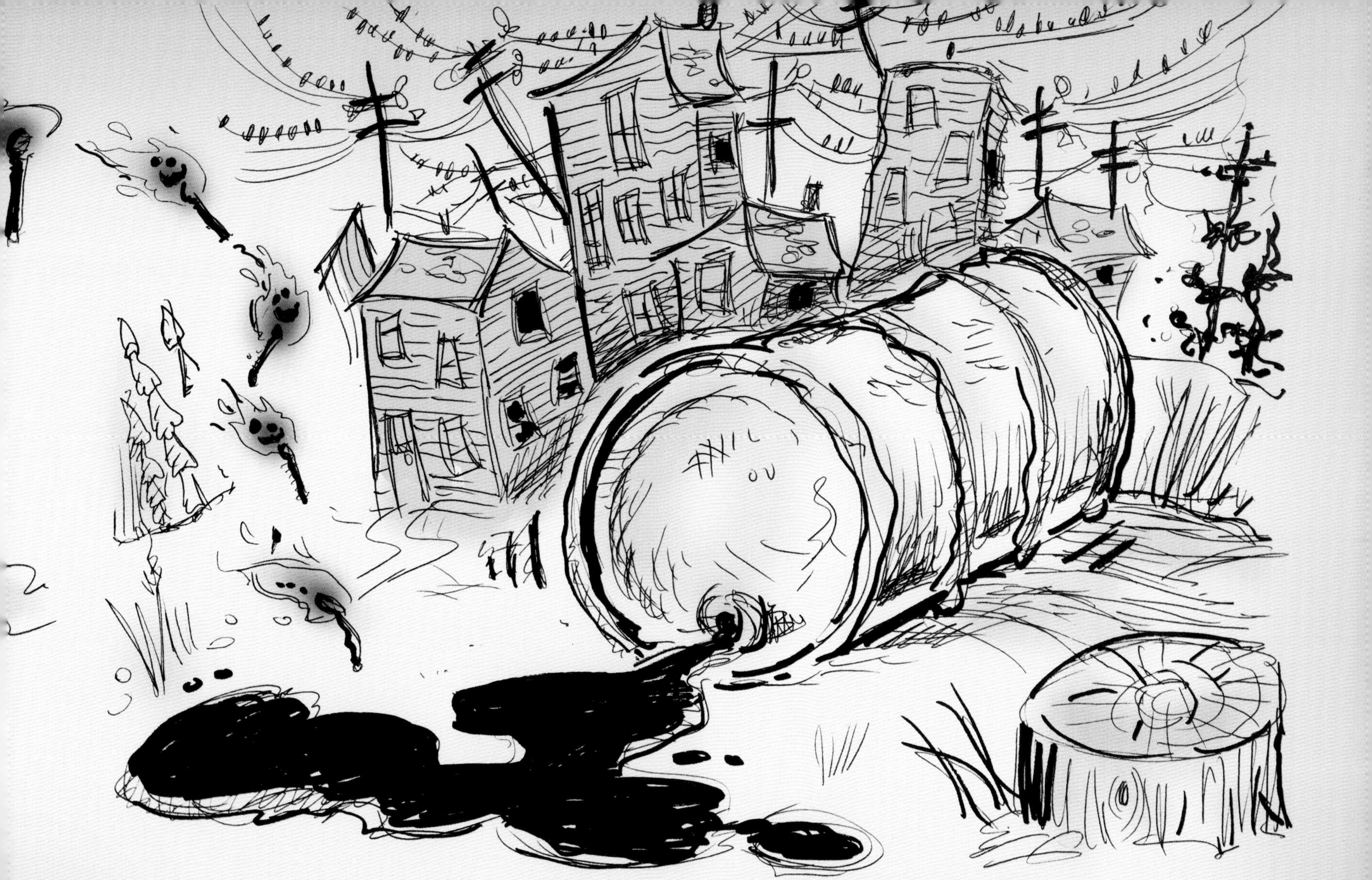

Lightin' up a smoke he laid the chainsaw down
Said "I'm the guy who saved your town"
Then Earle knocked over a drum of gas
Just as he threw away his match

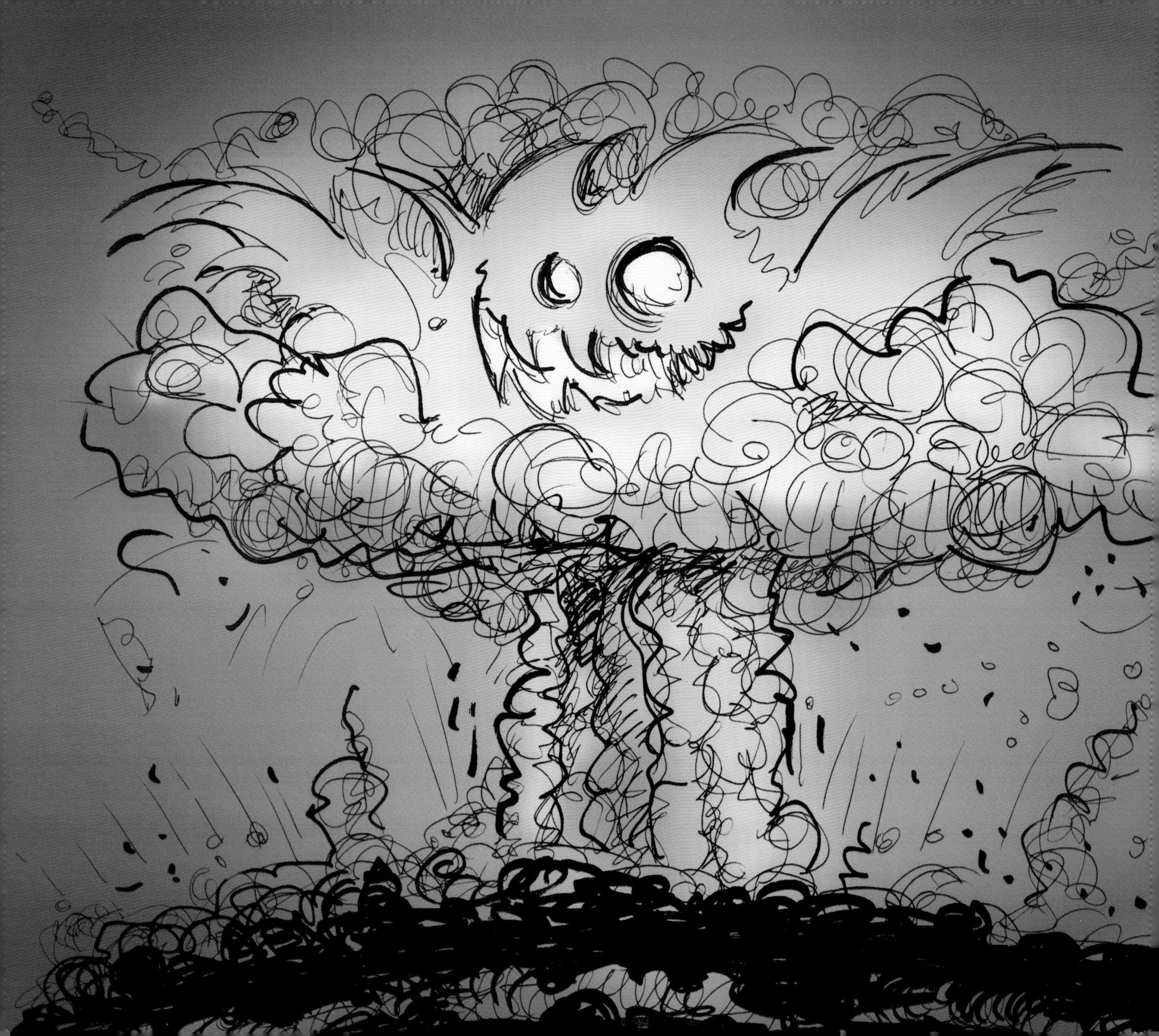

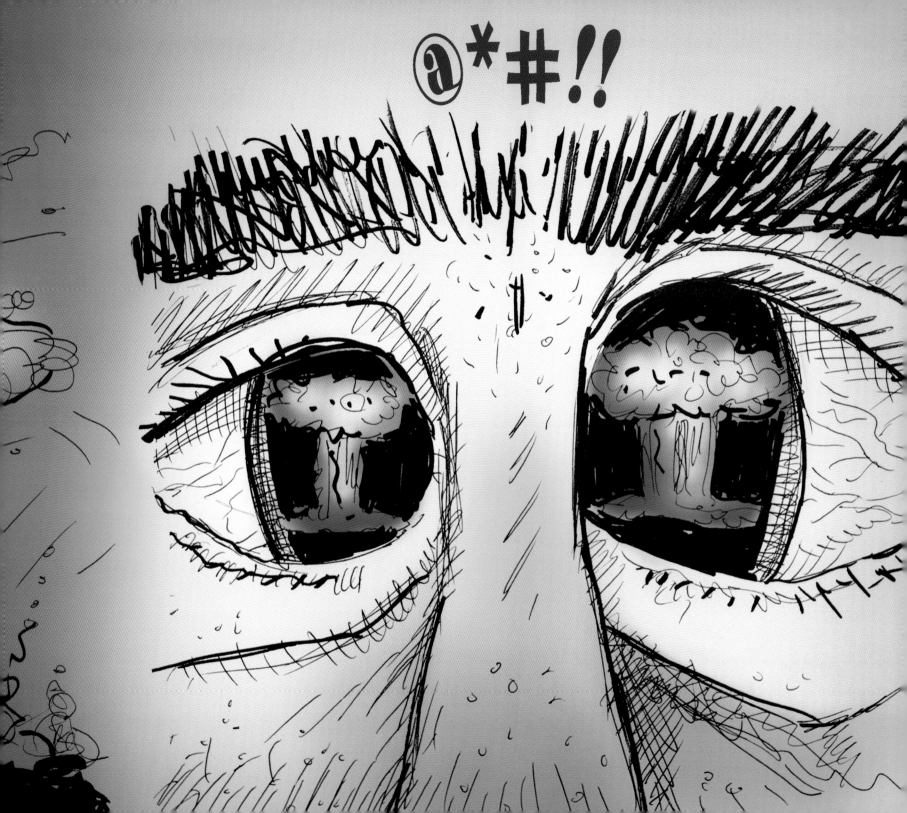

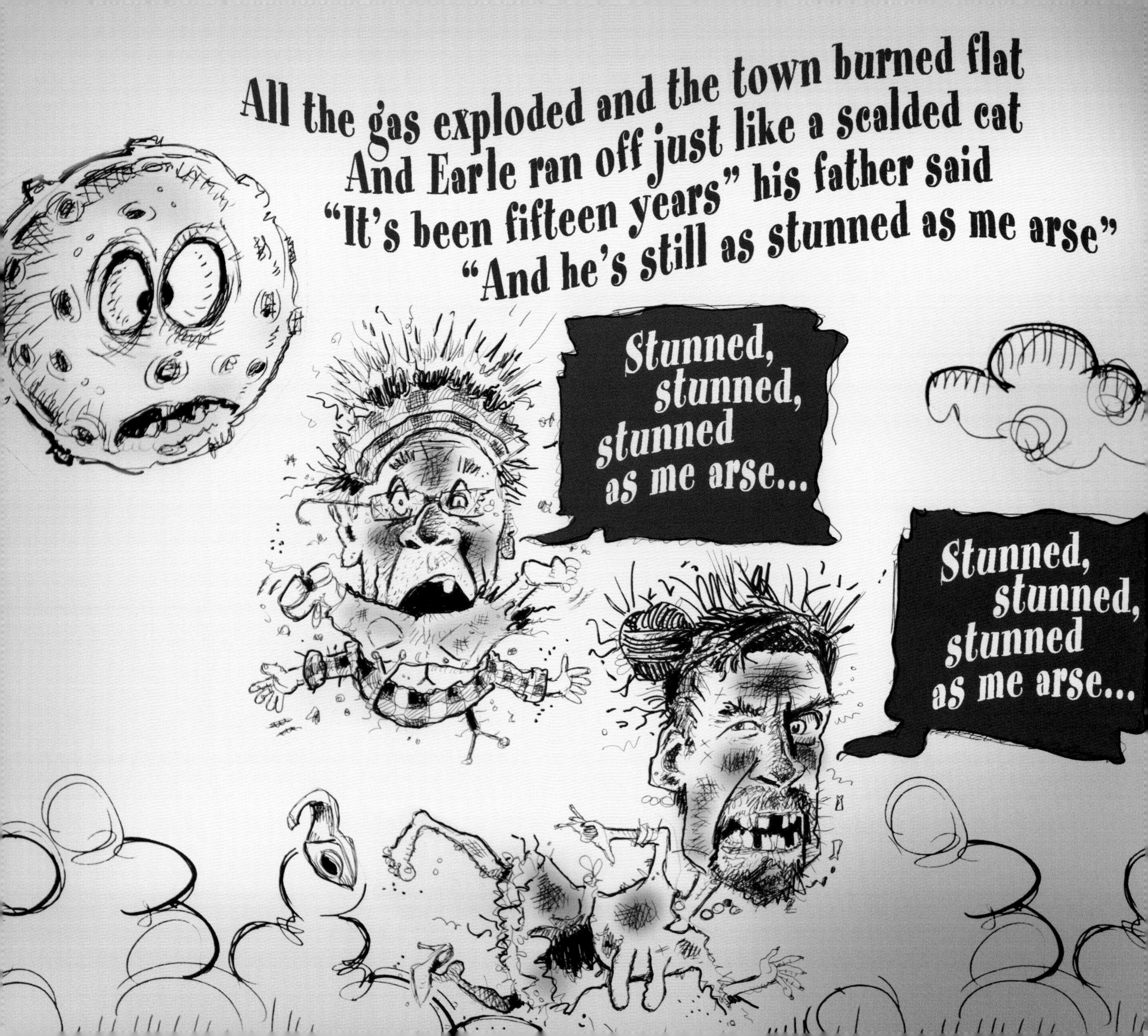
All the gas exploded and the town burned flat
And Earle ran off just like a scalded cat
"It's been fifteen years" his father said
"It's been fifteen years" his father said
"And he's still as stunned as me arse"
Stunned, stunned, stunned as me arse...
Stunned, stunned, stunned as me arse...

Stunned, stunned,
stunned as me arse,
Was Earle.

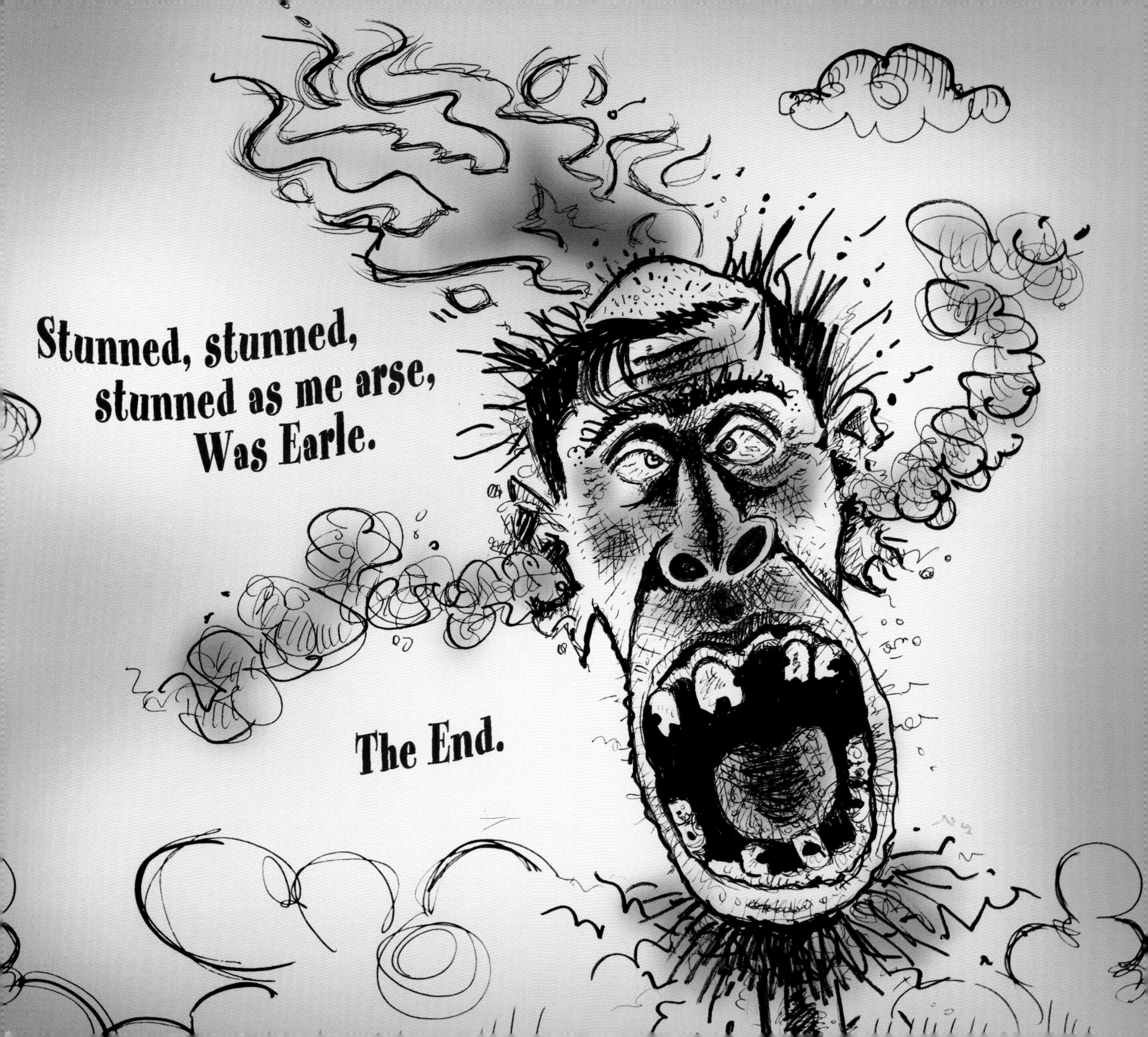

The End.

A Wayne Chaulk/Kevin Tobin Production

Written by Kevin Blackmore and Wayne Chaulk, Buddy Wasisname and the Other Fellers
Illustrated by Kevin Tobin (KT.)

Art Direction by Derek Mills and Heather Haggett
Special thanks to Donna Francis and Creative Book Publishing, for all your assistance and support.

BUDDY WASISNAME AND THE OTHER FELLERS...

In 1983, Ray Johnson, Wayne Chaulk and Kevin Blackmore met. Having spent time playing for enjoyment,
the trio found themselves in the summer of '85 playing a ten-day stint at the Newfoundland and Labrador pavilion
of Toronto Caravan, a festival celebrating the city's multiculturalism. They were part of an effort that won the
Caravan's Best Entertainment award. Things grew until weekends got cluttered doing concerts, and summers
were taken up with touring. By 1987, they abandoned all previous occupations and collectively "went at it!"
The trio has toured in every province and territory in Canada for more than twenty-seven years.

Ray Johnson, Job's Cove, Conception Bay, NL

Sings, plays the accordion and fiddle, assists with the song and recitation writing, contributes a large number
of traditional songs, and plays a great straight man in comic routines. Ray is well known as a brilliant instrumentalist.

Wayne Chaulk, Charlottetown, Bonavista Bay, NL

Sings, plays the guitar and mandolin, and does a large part of the formal script writing. He does straight man parts
as well as characters in the skits. He writes both comic and straight songs and is well known for his contemplative
ballads.

Kevin Blackmore, Glovertown, Bonavista Bay, NL

Sings, creates noise and acts like a loon with rabies. Contributes to the song and comedy writing and plays guitar,
mandolin, bass, banjo and almost anything capable of producing sound if squeezed, shot, banged or broken.
He should be contained at all times.

...AND ANOTHER FELLER

Kevin Tobin (KT.), Conception Bay South, NL

Can't sing, can't play nothin', but he can draw! Editorial cartoonist for The Telegram in St. John's for more than
twenty years. Published ten books of his cartoons. **Chainsaw Earle** is his first illustrated project with Wayne Chaulk
and Buddy Wasisname and the Other Fellers.